RESCUE ONE DOWN

JOHN M. MILLER

Tonka Bay Books

ISBN: 979-8-9918729-0-4

DEDICATION

This book is dedicated to teens everywhere who have the courage to reach deep within and use that power to be a positive force for good in our world. An act of kindness, however small or seemingly insignificant, has the potential to be life-changing, yes, even heroic. Your daringness to step forth has the potential to remind us as adults of a behavior we have long forgotten to embrace.

I'm fortunate to watch two such young men develop that courage.

ACKNOWLEDGMENTS

Rescue One Down is a work of fiction. Although actual places are described herein, the author has taken the liberty to adapt them to fit the story. Any semblance of the events and characters to persons, living or dead or life happenings is purely coincidental.

Thank you to Jim for work on the beta copy and Matthew, for assistance with the graphics. Their help and insights were invaluable in the publication of this novel.

Authors often 'zone out' when writing, many times to the detriment of a spouse. I'm grateful Sandy has provided the space and time within our busy lives for this part of our adventure together.

JMM

For Isaac & Henry

Prologue

On the road, the weather turned ugly. Lightning was illuminating the gray cloud shrouded sky. Even though it was the middle of the afternoon, the impending storm created a darkness equivalent to hours after sunset. As the pickup pulling the tent-trailer arrived at St. Croix State Park campground, the storm was gathering in intensity. The four heard the tornado sirens wailing. Although the boys had grown up hearing the usual tornado siren tests that authorities regularly conducted, they had never experienced an actual tornado firsthand. Their grandfather's pickup truck was shaking as the increase in the strength of the rain and wind buffeted it. The threat suddenly became real as they sensed the impending danger of the storm. There was no doubt, from the looks on the adult's faces, this was not simply a practice drill. They needed to find safety, and fast.

One

Months earlier...

It was February when the calendars were laid out on the dining table. June dates were selected for the second annual camping trip to St. Croix State Park in Northeastern Minnesota. The trip wasn't scheduled for months, but the two brothers, Nathan, who liked to go by Nate and Patrick, started dreaming about the end of snow and the warm temps of summer. They envisioned fishing for smallmouth bass from a canoe on the St. Croix River, and hiking the pathways through the woods, all in one of Minnesota's largest state parks. They laughed as they thought about making hobo meals, throwing the tin foil packets into the fire, hoping that everything inside the packet was edible and not burned to something unrecognizable. If all else failed, the s'mores were always a good failsafe way to stem the hunger.

The family tent trailer was old and well worn, used by both the parents and grandparents throughout the years. The shell was pock marked from hailstorms and the tent fabric had seen better days.

It was very different in a Malibu home in California along the coast. Katrina Edwards and her parents sat around the supper table discussing where to take their brand spanking new 39' fifth wheel pull behind RV. There was no pretense that the family was going to be roughing it on this trip in their $100,000 trailer. The RV had room to sleep six, laundry, a kitchen with an island, a primary suite with a king-size bed, a couple of bathrooms and a bunk room. It had twin air-conditioning units, and a full-blown 35,000 Btu furnace system. Not to be left out was the entertainment area with a 50" tv.

Mrs. Edwards, Ella, had seen a magazine advertisement about the lakes and forests in Minnesota. She suggested they test out the RV at one of those Minnesota state parks half-way across the country. Bob, Katrina's dad, researched the available RV state park sites. Finding everything already reserved in the parks between Duluth and the

Canadian border, they landed on St. Croix State Park as an acceptable compromise. If they were tired of the woods, they could drive north an hour or so and be in the city of Duluth, or south and be at the Mall of America in Minneapolis in a couple of hours. The description of the park sounded like it would have plenty to do to hold the interest of a teen daughter. Katrina, however, wasn't so certain, and begged her parents to allow her bestie, Elizabeth, to come along on the multi-week trip to the Midwest.

The months passed quickly. The end of the school year marked the beginning of the adventure to the Minnesota park for Katrina and Elizabeth. Both had their faces in their phones and iPads day after day as the four headed across the country. Katrina was already missing the beach after the first hours in the car. She normally spent her summer vacation on a surfboard in a wet suit. Elizabeth, who could hold her own on a surfboard, was more into soccer. She played goalie on her traveling team and stayed current on the missed practices and games by texting her teammates.

Each night, at the various stops along the way to Minnesota, it became easier for Bob to park and set up the RV as he became more familiar with the process. He was careful around the RV, not wanting to put a scratch on his pride and joy.

They finally pulled into St. Croix State Park about four o'clock on Tuesday. The weather was beautiful. Seventy–five degrees and sunny, with a few wispy clouds floating overhead. Katrina and Elizabeth unpacked their bikes first thing and rode around the park's paved trails, getting a feel for the place. They rode until they came to the river overlook. They instantly realized they wanted to spend as much time as possible on and exploring the river. It was beautiful.

That evening they went to the nightly ranger talk in the Campground lodge. When they had checked in at the ranger station earlier in the day, they picked up a schedule of the ranger talks for each evening. The program for that night was advertised as 'Missing Treasures'.

Elizabeth and the Edwards family found seats at a picnic table in the large log structure that had obviously been well used by years of campers. The duty ranger for the program was Hugh Anderson. He introduced himself as the lead ranger at St. Croix St. Park. He explained his job was to make certain the campers had a wonderful experience in the State Park and provide everyone with information about the flora and fauna of the area.

The talk of the evening was about Black Bears and an attack on a camper the first summer of the state park's existence back in 1943. The story provided by the ranger explained that the camper that was attacked had stolen 48 rare silver dollar coins from a famous collector in the Twin Cities. He drove north to the state park with his loot, intending to hide out from the cops. It would be the last place, he thought, that the authorities would look for him. He stored the coins in a leather pouch, which he tied closed with a couple of leather strings.

"Unfortunately, the thief wasn't much of a camper, nor did he pay any attention to the fact that he was in bear country. He stopped in Hinckley and bought a sack of groceries. He came to the campground, put up a tent and promptly brought the groceries into his canvas shelter.

"Staff rangers have passed down the story surrounding the event at these evening talks for over 80 years. It is now difficult to separate the fact from what has become legend. We know the man was in the tent making himself a peanut butter sandwich when a black bear wandered into the campground. Immediately smelling the food in the tent, the bear took a swipe at the tent with his enormous paw, ripping the tent and surprising the coin thief.

"Here's where the story gets murky. We think the man made the fatal mistake by deciding to do battle with the bear. Instead of running, he tried to scare off the bear. The bear was unsympathetic to the antics of the man eventually mauling him to death.

"After the authorities investigated and determined the identity of the man and what he had done, they began looking for the stolen coins. The fact of the matter is that the coins disappeared that day in 1943 and have never been found. Authorities on the scene believed someone heard the commotion, saw the dead man and took the bag of coins.

"The legend passed down is more interesting. After the bear killed the camper and ate the peanut butter sandwich, he ran back off into the woods. What happened to the coins? Remember the coin bag tied with strings? As a result of destroying the tent and the man occupying it, the bear accidentally entangled the strings of the bag around the long, sharp claws on one of its paws. The bag thus traveled off into the woods with the bear. The bear shook himself free from the bag of coins someplace in the forest. No one knows exactly where. As the legend goes, that bag of rare coins awaits discovery by a lucky camper here in St. Croix State Park.

"I tell the story tonight to excite you about discovering all the richness of this beautiful park. Yes, there's a small possibility that one of you can leave the campground with some newfound wealth by finding the coins. But more importantly, I want to remind everyone that this is bear country and to never ever have any food in your tent. Yes, the bear population around here is smaller than it was in the 1940s, but bears are still in the area and wander into the campground. So please don't entice the wildlife in the same manner as the coin thief.

"So, skip the bear encounter and instead get close up and personal with a bear claw pastry at Tobies in Hinckley. And as you scarf down the delicious pastry, remember the 1943 episode of the black bear and the 48 missing coins."

Two

Because of Jay McPherson's work schedule, it was Wednesday morning before when sons, Nate, and Patrick's second trip to the park was finally underway. It differed greatly from that of the family in the California RV and had quite the process to get things in order to head out. Sleeping bags, coolers, fishing equipment, bikes, ruck sacks with clothes and food for four hungry campers had to be loaded into the pickup and tent trailer. By early afternoon, the sunny skies had given way to clouds and what looked like some serious showers. The on- the- road portion would only take a few hours since the boys and their parents lived in one of the Western suburbs of Minneapolis, called Golden Valley.

Nate was into fishing, thus making certain several rods and his tackle box were securely packed in the truck. He wore his team's baseball hat with a logo that had a large GV over the top of it. His strong, accurate arm often put him in the positions of shortstop and pitcher. He lamented the fact that he would miss several games, but his love for fishing softened the blow. He was ready for the river.

Patrick for the past couple of years had been in a growth spurt, not only gaining height but also filling in with muscle. His life, both at school and after, revolved around football and basketball. During the summers, he worked out for several hours early in the morning at school and then spent the evenings in drills and scrimmages with his teammates. Basketball games consumed every weekend. Patrick often found himself in a leadership position in both sports, quarterback on the field and point guard on the court. Although he loved the wilderness, missing basketball was going to be hard on him.

Mom, Carole, was more of a luxury hotel type person than a tent trailer type camper. She wished hubby, Jay, and the boys well as they headed out the door. Their grandfather, Albert, stored the tent trailer at his hobby farm about forty-five minutes' drive from Golden Valley in a bedroom community called

Waconia. The farm was much more than a farm; it was often a training or retreat center for other agents.

Grandpa Al lived an unusual life in his retirement. He had served for many years as a special agent with the Department of Homeland Security. Prior to retirement, he was on a short list of agents who would be called for the most difficult situations. His boss was in a Washington, DC, office and was constantly in touch with the President of the United States. In retirement, Gramps, as the boys called him, did some moonlighting.

Three

What a difference 24 hours makes. The Edwards family arrived at St. Croix State Park on a beautiful, sunny afternoon. The McPhersons were not so lucky. Driving North on Interstate 35, the weather turned ugly. Lots of lightning filled the dark gray skies. News bulletins broke into the regular radio programming warning of the possibility of tornadoes and, at the very least, severe storms. About ten miles from the state park, the storm looked ominous, and the sky took on a greenish gray color. Rain came down in sheets. The two brothers thought it looked pretty cool. Two adults in the truck, not so much.

The pounding rain and strong winds buffeted the pickup truck. As the four pulled off the highway and drove through the large stone pillars that formed the gateway to the park, a large pine tree crashed onto the road about 50 yards in front of the pickup. Fortunately, most of the tree landed to the side of the road, leaving one lane still passable. Although Gramps slowed the pickup to go around the tree, both boys noticed another uptick in the two adult's level of concern. Gramps pushed down the accelerator and the truck and the tow-behind camper trailer increased in speed, hoping to find safety in a park building. They passed a sign, 'Camp Office' two miles ahead.

Gramps said to the other three, "We have to find a tornado-proof building and find it quickly." Upon arrival at the office, Jay ran to check in and learn where the safest buildings were.

The ranger on duty was short with him. "Check in later. Go immediately straight ahead to the lodge building. It's the safest place for miles around. We're under a tornado warning. Go now."

Jay was disappointed to hear there was not a secure underground facility for severe storm protection for the public. Likely, there were hundreds of people camping in the park at the time.

The lodge came into view within minutes' drive. The ranger from the camp office was right behind them. Campers were scurrying from all directions, heading to the old log building to seek shelter from the storm. Grandpa Al silently hoped it could handle this one. Upon entering, they found campers of every age and size wet, cold, and afraid crammed into the one room lodge.

The three on duty rangers, two males and a female, were part of the contingent of people seeking shelter in the lodge. Tornado sirens continued to blare in the background. Nathan and Patrick huddled under one of the log style tables while Grandpa Al and father, Jay sat on a bench at that same table. Loud screams poured out of the mouths of young children at the sound of an unknown explosion. In actuality, it was a 100-year-old tall pine which scraped the lodge wall as it cascaded towards earth.

Gramps admitted to Jay and the boys that in all his years on the earth he had never been directly in the path of a tornado. The tornados had always devastated other areas. But it looked like that was going to change as suddenly the wind increased significantly, sounding like an out-of-control freight train pounding down the tracks. But there were no

tracks outside the lodge. A ranger yelled, "take cover, the tornado is here!"

The lodge creaked as the roof shingles peeled away from the structure. Rangers in the lodge were yelling at the top of their lungs for everyone to cover their heads as debris and water started raining down on the lodge guests as parts of the roofing were torn away. Loud crashing sounds mixed in with the pelting of debris hitting the lodge's exterior only added to the terror that was being experienced.

The log structure groaned but stayed upright. Although it seemed like it was at least a half hour, in reality, the tornado was only on the ground for minutes before lifting itself skyward, leaving the destruction in its wake. The park had experienced a direct hit by the tornado. It would be a day or two before the national weather service officially defined the strength of the tornado based on the Fujita Scale.

The same ranger that had yelled 'tornado here' wore the name tag, Hugh Anderson. He slowly opened the three-inch-thick, solid wood lodge door. The rain continued to fall, but the freight train sounding wind had diminished. Gradually, the campers exited the lodge building. What they saw was unimaginable. Cars were turned on their sides and thrown into what was left of the trees by the hurricane-force winds. Everywhere, the tall pines were snapped in half. The tents were no more, every one of them completely gone, including everything that was in them.

The RV portion of the campground looked like a bunch of little toys that someone had accidentally kicked about with their foot. Downed trees had crushed several of the RVs. The Edwards $100,000 RV had survived, but had broken windows, and was dented on every surface from the wind driven projectiles. A tree branch penetrated the aluminum skin of their RV. They would go nowhere for the foreseeable future. Trees were down around their new pickup, effectively blocking it from moving anywhere. It looked like their RV was 50 years old and had been through a war rather than brand new. Many other RV units were not so lucky. They were turned over on their side or destroyed when their aluminum shells were peeled away like that of an onion.

As the width and breadth of the destruction came to be realized, adults and children began to cry and hug their parents. Everywhere campers were trying to use their cell phones for help. It was a fruitless endeavor. The tornado had taken down the only cell tower miles away. In fact, there was no longer any electricity to the campground or surrounding areas. They were effectively isolated from the outside world.

Four

The four McPhersons exited the lodge together. There was upheaval and commotion everywhere, but screaming from the nearby RV area captured their attention. Mr. and Mrs. Edwards had not heeded the ranger's call to go to the lodge, deciding instead to ride out the storm in their new RV. They figured their expensive investment was built to take on any storm. Both parents had grown up in California and had really never paid attention to tornados. They identified more with forest fires, mudslides, and earthquakes, which wreaked havoc on their state regularly.

There was a second reason they stayed with the RV. It was the more important reason. They were missing the two teens they had brought with them. Not only was their daughter missing, but they were responsible for their daughter's friend as well. They hoped by staying in the RV, their teens would somehow show up even in the midst of the storm.

But it was not to be. Two rangers, Hugh, and the female ranger, Alice Harrison, started running toward the man and woman who were screaming, "Our daughter is missing!" As the rangers approached, they poured out their hearts. "She was out biking with a girlfriend before the tornado blew through." The boys overheard the parents telling the ranger that the girl's names were Elizabeth and Katrina. The teens left after lunch to go exploring. They were supposed to be back in three hours to their fancy RV. The girls never showed up and then the tornado hit. "They only took a bottle of water with them. I don't think they even had jackets because it was warm when they left. Katrina has long blonde hair and blue eyes. She's 5'4" and 15 years old. Elizabeth has brunette hair and brown eyes. She's a little shorter than Katrina and 14 years old," said Mrs. Edwards.

Ranger Hugh Anderson suddenly went numb. It was unimaginable. Two teenage girls missing in a land of debris and destruction. He tried to calm the parents down, but they were beyond consolable. Anderson had been a ranger for 10 years and had helped campers out of tight jams many times. However, what stood out in his mind were not the successful conclusions, but the failed attempts at helping.

The one event that stood in front and center in his mind, even though it happened years prior, was an incident where a young brother and sister had been involved. Without the parent's knowledge, the two, ages 10 and 11, had wandered down to the river, stolen a canoe and set out to explore the river. Unfortunately, their canoe capsized and without life jackets, they had no hope of winning the struggle against the current and cold of the river. It took local law enforcement, the entire ranger staff, including the off-duty rangers, 24 hours before they found the missing children. Ranger Anderson made the discovery and had to tell the parents the awful news. It was every parent's worst nightmare.

Anderson would never forget that day. In talking with Edwards, he made no promises other than they would all do their best to find their teens. Because it was mid-week, only three rangers were on duty for the whole campground, now with communications down, roads blocked with trees and no electricity anywhere in the area, Anderson knew one ranger was going to have to attend to the campers who were trying to make heads and tails out of the destruction. At most, he and another ranger would be available to search. He told Ranger Alice to stay at the office. He and ranger Chuck Clausen would lead the search. It was an impossible task, considering the vast areas of the state park. The only hope would be to enlist as many of the campers as he could to help search for the missing girls.

Five

There was upheaval and disarray in every direction in the campground. Campers were crying, having lost everything. Many were wandering around in the rain looking for anything that was familiar. Some were helping calm others who were distraught.

Al McPherson had parked the pickup and tent trailer in the lot across from the lodge. By sheer luck, they had parked behind the camp store. Smaller than the lodge, it too was a log structure that was damaged, but still upright after the storm. It had been substantial enough to provide some protection to the vehicles in the lot from the tornado. McPherson's camper was flipped over on to its side, ripped from the truck trailer hitch. It was battered, but was still in one piece. The pickup truck was pock marked everywhere; the front windshield was seriously cracked. The back window wasn't so lucky. A branch now protruded through the opening where glass had previously existed.

Unlike many in the campground, the McPherson family was relatively calm. Grandpa Al, now retired, had been a decorated special agent with Homeland Security. In the years since his retirement, he made his farm available to active Homeland Security personnel to help them through post-traumatic stress disorder, commonly known as PTSD. Agents often struggled with PTSD because of the difficult situations they had to deal with. Likewise, the farm was also used to guide agents with further training.

Al McPherson was more than respected. His peers and the upcoming generation of agents considered him a hero. His son, Jay, was not enamored with his father's profession. Assignments took Albert away from his family. In fact, Jay was bitter. His father had missed many of his high school soccer games, graduation, and a whole host of birthdays. Even college graduation was missed by his father because of an agency assignment. The years since had smoothed the waters to a degree, but he continued to feel the agency had robbed him of several important moments in his life.

Al knew all too well that he had been less than a good father. Now he was determined to make up ground by spending time with his grandsons, Patrick, and Nathan. He started teaching them a simplified version of the agency's curriculum when they were young elementary school students. It ranged from survival skills to tracking, to knife and gun handling pointers. Much of this training went unnoticed by their parents because the boys would head out to the farm to spend the weekends with grandma and grandpa. By the time Patrick was 15 and Nathan 14, they not only could give gramps a run for his money with their skills, they also had developed a confidence within themselves that they could handle difficult situations.

Grandpa Al had taught them to use their skills for betterment, whether it be to offer first aid or an understanding ear to someone struggling at school. They learned both defensive strategies and rescue basics. One of the important, if not the most important, skill they were taught was to 'be prepared'. Gramps talked to them about the importance of being well prepared and how that influenced the outcome in difficult circumstances. They learned their school backpacks were the perfect vehicle to carry things that normally wouldn't fit in their pockets. They came to learn what necessities were and what things were niceties to have in those backpacks. Gradually, they understood the benefits of 'packing for the situations you might encounter'. That teaching held true for going camping as well. Gramps was proud of the two. They were going to be truly fine young men.

Six

Rangers Anderson and Harrison continued to meet with Mr. and Mrs. Edwards about the two missing teens, trying to learn what they were wearing, where they liked to explore, and what their bikes looked like. While professing to develop a search plan, the rangers knew they had almost zero chance of finding the girls alive after the extremely destructive tornado. Bob said, "I bought Katrina a new Specialized Crux Comp bike just before we left California. The color is Arctic Blue. I rented the same Specialized one for Elizabeth. Hers is smoke color."

Nate and Patrick went to their overturned tent trailer seeking to convince dad to let them go looking for the girls. Dad, of course, was not hot on the idea. "Boys, it's nice of you to be concerned about those two girls, but really the rangers are so much better equipped to look for them. And not only that, it's going to be dark soon. Besides, there's no cell phone service, so we can't even stay in contact with you," argued Dad.

Patrick, the elder of the two, looked at Gramps and then dad, "I know we're just kids, but I think we have some skills to at least help in the search. And we'll stay together. Don't worry about us, dad, right, gramps?"

Grandpa Al finally jumped to the aid of the boys. "I agree with the boys. I think they could help in the search even in the dark. They already know the park from camping here last year and they both have compasses and know how to use them. I think the worst that might happen is that they would get drenched in the rain and cold as the temps drop tonight. Besides, it looks like the rangers need every extra body they can find to help with the search."

Dad finally relented, and the boys put on their raincoats and their well-equipped backpacks. Water, snacks, a pocketknife, compass, headlamp, fire starter, first aid supplies, and sweatshirts were included as part of the backpack inventory.

Before heading to assess the damage to the camping trailer and pickup, the boys had listened to a portion of the Edwards conversation with the rangers. Elizabeth and Katrina had been on bikes when they had left earlier in the day and had disappeared. The boys told Dad and Gramps they were going to go to the end of the trail and work their way back to the campground. Patrick told the two adults that they shouldn't worry because they probably would spend most of the night searching. Dad was still hesitant, instructing them to come back to the campground when they were tired or low on supplies.

As the two headed out on their own mountain style bikes, they hoped against hope of finding the girls. As they set out, they talked about the cost of a Specialized Crux Comp bike. Patrick thought he saw them advertised for something like $5000 each. Nate couldn't imagine two wheels costing that much.

"Hey, it should be a piece of cake to find those bikes. For that kind of money, they probably have glow in the dark paint and locator beacons on them. How hard can it be?" asked Patrick.

Dad and gramps promised the boys they too would also join the search as soon as they could find their hiking boots and rain jackets.

"If I was out in that blasted wind and was going to survive the tornado, I would have gone over the bank and hidden somewhere under a fallen tree of something," said Nate.

"Would you have done that if gramps hadn't taught us those survival skills?" asked Patrick.

"I think so. It might be almost the only response with the strength of the wind. They would want to get away from it and about the only place to hide is over the riverbank or a really deep ditch and I recall nothing like that out there," came the reply from the younger brother.

"Ok, then, let's find the bikes and then go over the bank and start searching," said Patrick as they both started pedaling down the paved biking trail.

Seven

The paved bike paths that the girls most likely would have used were now blocked by large, downed trees. It would be impossible for the ranger 4-wheelers to get anywhere using the pathway. Anyone searching would have to go on foot after encountering the first tree blocking the path. Patrick and Nate, however, were able to carry their bikes between and over the limbs and to continue riding until they encountered the next obstacle. Eventually, they were miles from the lodge. Everywhere they looked, there were tons of debris, downed trees, and major limbs on the ground. In large swaths, not a single pine tree remained standing. The obliteration of the forest was complete.

Witnessing the destruction firsthand, they began to think that no one could ever survive being outside in the tornado. Another reality entered the picture. There were so many trees on the ground that there was very little hope that they would find the girls' bikes. It became apparent the bikes were either completely blown away or buried under the branches of the hundreds and hundreds of enormous trees that were lying on the ground.

The guys began to believe the missing girls must have been miles from the campground when the storm struck. Otherwise, why wouldn't they have made it back to their RV when the sirens went off announcing the impending tornado? The more they thought about the distance factor, the more they were convinced they needed to keep trucking towards the end of the trail system.

Progress was extremely slow. They rode for a minute and then be off their bikes, trying to carry and walk their bikes around the fallen tree that was in their way on the path. As the hours passed, they talked about heading back to the campground to find dad and grandpa. It had taken them two hours of slow progress in what had started out as dusk, now had faded into profound darkness. Reaching the end of the trail, they left their bikes on the path and searched on foot. They knew there was about a zero chance someone would wander all the way down the pathway to steal their expensive mountain-style bikes. They decided their best chance of finding the girls would be to walk the riverbank back to the campground. It would not be easy in the dark.

They would have to fight the myriads of downed trees, brambles and the ever-present poison ivy. The steepness of the bank and the slippery slopes caused by the rain were going to make it a miserable hike back to the campground. The guys calculated the river was about 75 feet straight down. With the continuous rain, the water level of the river was extremely high. The usual beach shoreline was now non-existent. If someone was to fall while on the slope, they would likely roll their way down into the river.

Nate and Patrick crawled, straddled, and pulled their bodies over the blown down trees that littered the riverbank, creating the major obstacle course for the two brothers. They pretended to be new recruits for the navy seals. How much worse could it be? The battery-operated headlamps were helping to a degree by providing a small swath of light, especially with the rain pouring down. Fortunately, it was enough for the guys to see what was directly in front of them.

After another forty-five minutes of moving at a snail's pace, constantly yelling out the girls' names at the top of their lungs, they heard something. They weren't certain what the sound was. At first, they reckoned it was an injured animal. They had seen several dead animals, including a large buck that a fallen tree partially covered. The pouring rain, the thunder muffled the unusual sound. At first, it sounded like a soft whimper.

Hearing it again spurred Patrick to yell as loud as he could, "Elizabeth, Katrina!"

"Over here!" came the reply, barely audible above the noise of the onslaught of wind and rain.

As they turned their heads toward the voices, their headlamps illuminated two soaked, shivering girls in their short sleeve tops and shorts. One girl was holding the other's head in her lap. There was a huge tree branch partially covering them.

"Help us please! I think she has a broken leg," said Katrina. "The tree fell on us as we were trying to get back to camp. Where are the rangers? Are you with them?"

"No, we came searching for you on our own." The girls' hopes took a nosedive when they heard there weren't any adults with them. For a moment, they thought rescuers had found them and would take them back to the campground. But it was not to be.

They introduced themselves. The girls looked nothing like what Nate and Patrick had in their minds. In the light from their headlamps they looked like drowned rats, their wet hair matted to their faces. Elizabeth was crying. It didn't take a rocket scientist to know that her pain was coming from the huge branch laying across her legs. Nate and Patrick tried to lift the large branch off Elizabeth. In reality, it was a very heavy log. The best the guys could do was to lift it up about one-half an inch, far too little to be of help.

They searched for something they could use as a lever, creating a kind of fulcrum to raise the log. Eventually, Nate found a long branch that he pulled over to the trapped Elizabeth. It looked like it was perfect for what they needed. The guys were hopeful, but uncertain they could move the log. Katrina's job was to pull Elizabeth free when and if they moved the log. The first few attempts proved to be fruitless. After repositioning of their lever multiple time, some grunting and groaning, they raised the log up four inches. But it was enough to free Elizabeth. It was a good sign of hope, but they were a long way from being home free.

Eight

The wind was still blowing, the rain still coming down. It was pitch black on the riverbank. Elizabeth was still crying in pain even after she was extracted from under the log. Katrina was trying in vain to calm her down. Patrick shouted above the storm, "Elizabeth, we're here to help you, but you have to tell us where it hurts."

She pointed to her lower legs, one or possibly both. As part of their training, the boys carried basic first aid supplies in their backpacks. But in this instance, they knew they were not equipped to do much with a broken leg or maybe two.

With their headlamps focused on Elizabeth's legs, they could see the major bruise marks. They decided the safest thing would be to make splints to immobilize her legs, not knowing if the fallen tree's enormous branch had broken her legs. It would not be a simple decision or process in the rain. However, the splints would not be the most difficult part. There were branches everywhere. It was going to be the unknown of what was going to happen after that. Splinting the legs would mean there was going to be no way that she was going to move from this location. They were effectively sealing their fate to stay right where they were throughout the night or until rescuers showed up to help. Even if they could build some kind of makeshift stretcher to move her, there was no hope they could get the stretcher up the steep riverbank covered by downed trees and broken branches.

Worse than anything, Patrick noticed Elizabeth's breathing was becoming difficult and shallow. As he was wrapping her legs with gauze bandage to keep the splints in place, he could feel her skin was cold and clammy. At first, he chalked up to the chilly rain that was falling and the fact that she had been lying on the cold ground. But Elizabeth began to make statements that made no sense to anyone. Patrick guessed she was going into shock.

Katrina couldn't hear what Patrick and Nate were whispering to each other over the noise of the wind and rain. The guys were evaluating their options. They only came up with one. Hunker down and await daylight. A moment later, each pulled a dry sweatshirt out of their backpacks. Nate gave his to Katrina and told her to put it on quickly. Then Patrick told Katrina that she was going to have to help get the sweatshirt on Elizabeth. As soon as he and Nate lifted Elizabeth by the shoulders into a sitting position, she started screaming in pain. Katrina's job became next to impossible. She struggled not only because Elizabeth was screaming in pain, but she was also soaking wet, making it difficult to pull the sweatshirt on. Once they had Elizabeth in a dry sweatshirt, it was time to bring out the survival blankets.

Both of the guys had a twin pack of mylar survival blankets in their backpacks. It was the same thing that marathon runners were often wrapped in at the finish line in bad weather to help them retain body heat. Patrick and Nate had never used them before, but it was always something grandpa insisted they carry. Now they knew why. They spread the first on the ground and rolled Elizabeth on to it and completely wrapped her mummy style. The theory, according to gramps, was that the mylar would help to retain 90% of her body heat. To the guys, calling the piece of thin mylar a blanket seemed to be a misnomer, but hopefully it would do something to help them survive the cool night air.

With the potential that Elizabeth was going into shock, both boys realized the only thing they knew about it was that it could be life threatening. They thought they remembered something, on YouTube, or from Gramps that to minimize the effects of shock, they needed to turn Elizabeth's body so that her legs were slightly higher than her heart. Then it was time for the other three to get wrapped in survival blankets as well.

Katrina argued for going for help instead of sitting still in the rain on the steep bank. After all, the guys had flashlights that could help them find their way back. Patrick reminded her they would never be able to move Elizabeth up the steep slope and all the way back to the campground by themselves.

"Besides," said Patrick, "We're miles from the campground, with all pathways covered with downed trees. There's nothing safe about navigating right now. We'll be fine and safe here overnight. We can get help in the daylight."

Nine

The four were finally wrapped in mylar survival blankets. Unfortunately, life wasn't that great with the rain still coming down. Nate and Patrick were relatively dry with their rain jackets, but for the already soaked girls, the thin pieces of mylar were not enough. Patrick realized they needed protection from the rain. He had an idea. If they could huddle together, he would turn his blanket into a tarp. They used the downed tree branch that had imprisoned Elizabeth a short time earlier to support the new covering over them. Together, they pulled Elizabeth back under the cover of the branch and tarp.

Patrick wrapped gauze around the four corners of the mylar survival blanket turned tarp to hold it in place in the wind and rain. Elizabeth continued to cry softly. Neither Patrick nor Nate had ever been faced with a girl crying nonstop. Growing up, the guys only had each other, no girls except mom in the family. Nate tried to get her mind off the pain by offering a couple of energy bars from his backpack. They inhaled the bars. Both girls were more than starved, they had only water with them on their biking excursion. Once they all had something to eat, Nate and Patrick turned off their headlamps to conserve the batteries. It was going to be a long night. The boys knew in their hearts there was little likelihood that searchers would find them even if they happened by chance to anywhere in the area. There simply was no way to communicate with anyone.

Katrina, as the tarp began to magically shield the four from the rain, realized that she and Elizabeth were no longer alone on the slope of the riverbank. She also realized the guys had provided everything they needed to be okay, despite the really awful circumstances. In an interesting switch, the guys were becoming more pessimistic about the hours of darkness that still needed to be endured. They wondered to themselves if Elizabeth was going to be okay and if they should have split up, leaving two on the slope and the other two going for help. They wondered what was taking place with the bruises. Would Elizabeth make it through the night? They realized how helpless they were to do anything to help with potentially broken legs. The reality that Elizabeth was likely experiencing shock and not knowing how to do anything different to stave off more danger to her life was humbling.

Elizabeth surprised everyone when she blurted out, "this is by far the worst date I've ever been on". At first, the other three thought this was another of her statements that made little sense. Then they realized she was making a joke. It produced the desired reaction. All had a good laugh. Her attempt at humor was probably the best thing to happen. It instantly boosted the morale of the guys, now believing the patient was doing better. Even the crying stopped. Katrina had an idea. She touched Elizabeth's left ankle. "Do you feel anything? she asked Elizabeth.

"Ya, I feel your cold hand on my ankle." came the response. Katrina did the same to the right ankle. Again, the same answer from Elizabeth. Patrick silently noted the good sign. Katrina tried to do the humor thing as well. "Based on the ankle test, Elizabeth Jane McDonald, you're just faking it. No more sympathy for you."

"Oh sure, I suppose you want me to be like that guy in the Bible that Jesus told to pick up his bed and walk," responded Elizabeth. The other three groaned.

As the hours passed, the individuals on the dark river slope became a little less self-conscious and talked together more easily between themselves. The girls told Patrick and Nate they were from Malibu, California, on vacation in the park for only the second day. Patrick said he had seen Katrina's parents. They were okay and eager to find them. Katrina told the other three she was sorry she had disobeyed them by not being back within the three hours that they had authorized. Although no one could see it in the dark, tears were streaming down her cheeks as she thought about Elizabeth's legs and how worried her parents must be. Nate added that he and Patrick had just arrived at the campground with the onset of the tornado and that dad and grandpa would now be concerned but probably not worried sick.

Elizabeth perked up at that revelation and asked why the guy's parents wouldn't be out of their mind with worry after the storming, darkness, and lack of communication. Patrick stepped into answer Elizabeth, "Our grandpa has been teaching us for years how to be prepared for surprises on camping trips and in school. He has a large hobby farm, and we've spent a number of nights sleeping out under the stars by ourselves. Gramps would give us some kind of problem that we had to solve before we could come back to the farmhouse. He has helped us be confident that we can get through difficult stuff." He was careful to leave out of the discussion that grandpa was a retired agent and that he and Nate were trained in a lot more than surviving a night out in a storm. Gramps had drilled into them over and over; they were to keep the training details between themselves.

The girls told them about the ranger's talk about the bear and the stolen coins. Elizabeth admitted the coins had been on their minds and were the reason they were late in returning to the campground. They thought it would be fun to find the coins and be rich with the discovery. Nate wondered if the girls had any guesses on how many people had tried to find those coins in all the years since 1943.

Katrina changed the subject. "My parents bought this horrendously expensive RV that we towed to this campground. My dad had to buy a new pickup truck as well to pull the thing. You should see how he babies the trailer and the pickup. He won't hardly let us touch anything in it. He acted like it was the most important thing ever created. Every afternoon after we got parked in a campground along the way to Minnesota, he would walk around the RV checking to see if there were any new bugs splattered on the unit. He would get the spray bottle out and wash off each bug individually. It was really embarrassing. But dad has always been like that. As long as I can remember, everything was about money and nice things with him."

Neither Patrick nor Nate were willing to tell the girls about the destruction throughout the campground, which likely included that horrendously expensive RV. As the night dragged on, the rain finally stopped as while the four were talking about more personal things like their ages. Katrina said she had turned fifteen five months ago. Elizabeth was coming up to her 15th birthday. Patrick said he was looking forward to turning 16 soon, so he could get his driver's license. Nate discovered he was the youngest, still a few months behind Elizabeth.

The age revelations led to conversations ranging from what the girls liked to do after school in Malibu to the different AAU teams the guys played on all summer long. About 2:30 am, all four were losing their ability to keep their eyes open. The mylar blankets were helping to temper the cool night air, not quite making everyone feel toasty, but at least bearable. One after another dozed off, sometimes in the middle of a sentence. The first light of the new day was still hours away.

Nate was trying to get comfortable, laying on the wet slope. No matter which way he turned, something hard was jabbing him up near his shoulder. He tried to brush it out of the way, thinking it was a rock. As his hand touched the supposed rock, he realized it was something on edge sticking up out of the soil. It was thin and round shaped. He turned on his headlight and reached for the object. It wasn't a rock, but rather a coin half buried in the dirt. Nate couldn't believe it. He thought it might be an old silver dollar, so he stuck it in his pocket to be cleaned up later.

The four somehow found it possible to close their eyes and garner moments of sleep on the steep slope of the riverbank.

Ten

The evening scene back at the campground was chaotic at best, completely unreal at worst. There wasn't a camper whose possessions were not in some way or another untouched.

Down at the tent site section called the logging trail area, every single tent was completely blown away or shredded. There were pieces of fabric tangled in down tree branches. Soaked sleeping bags littered the campground. Cars that were parked at the individual campsites were either crushed by fallen trees or turned into large pieces of rubbish with windows blown out, branches protruding out of the windshields or sometimes, the cars were simply turned on their sides.

It was clear there was an attitude among the campers as they wandered around the area, looking for anything that might be salvageable. A Kindle was found under a branch, along with a children's stuffed giraffe laying under a picnic table turned on edge. A camp kit aluminum plate that became a flying saucer in the tornado was barely sticking out of the ground. The tent pole became an arrow and was found protruding out of the window frame on the restroom wall. And yet the campers exhibited an attitude of gratitude. Most had lost everything, yet as they wandered looking for their belongings, they seemed to care more about what their neighbor was missing. It was stranger helping stranger. The gratitude was, in essence, the realization that life was more important than possessions. They were thankful to be alive.

A female ranger with a loudspeaker appeared, obviously going throughout the campground on foot, making the same announcement several times. "Hello visitors! So far, it looks like there are only a few campers with superficial injuries from the tornado. However, we have two missing teenagers. We're enlisting volunteers to help with the search. If you can help meet Ranger Hugh at the lodge in 10 minutes. Bring flashlights if you have them. We will probably search 4 to 5 hours, so please bring your own water bottles as well.

"Even though we are without electricity, we are currently cleaning and setting up space in the lodge for everyone who doesn't have housing for the night. We are locating candles and flashlights. In the morning, we will be opening what is left of the camp store to provide whatever food was not destroyed in the storm at no charge to anyone. We hope the county will move the trees off our road tomorrow or soon thereafter to get aid to us. In the meantime, we need to all be patient."

Eleven

Park ranger Alice Harrison, a petite 5'2", young woman, third in command at the campground, was the only female ranger on duty that evening. Without communications between the rangers, she felt for maybe the first time all summer that she had no one to report to. She watched as Ranger Hugh and Ranger Chuck Clausen headed out with two groups of volunteer searchers to find the missing girls. Her job while they were out searching was to be the ranger in charge at the station. As the night went on, Alice felt semi-helpless. How many times could she tell campers she didn't know when help would come or when their cell phones would work again. She became restless with her inability to be of real help to anyone, including finding the lost girls.

There were no other rangers around to tell of her plan. She knew it was dangerous and that she could be risking her own life. But she also knew she could be fired for disobeying her boss. The 24-year-old ranger, usually very well put together, was looking disheveled from the long afternoon of the tornado and its aftermath as she walked away from her post at the ranger station to the campground maintenance garage.

She was in her second year of being on staff at St. Croix State Park. Following graduation from the University of Minnesota, Minneapolis campus, she applied and was hired as a ranger at St. Croix campground. Her primary job as a ranger was education. Alice figured she would spend a few years trying out the idea of being a ranger, and if she thought it held promise for a long-term career, she would enroll in the 16-week course required to add rescue and law enforcement to her educational capacity as a ranger. Tonight, she wished she had the rescue portion.

As she reached the maintenance building, she found the roof had been blown away, but there were still some walls standing. Inside, she found one of the 4-wheelers that the rangers used to get around the campground. She was surprised to find a full gas can behind an overturned workbench. She quickly strapped it to the backend of the 4-wheeler. A flashlight was on the floor. It was another one of those items she knew she needed. Alice almost did a cartwheel when she flipped on the switch. A bright white beam shone from the tube in her hand. She turned the key on the 4-wheeler and it started right away. A huge smile spread across her face. She was ready. As she pulled out of the roofless shed, she paused for a moment to re-think her decision to go off on her own to get help.

Her quickly formulated plan was to take the four-wheeler sixteen miles or more to the closest town of any size, Hinckley. She hoped there would be cell service in the town or, at a minimum, a working land line in order to call the closest law enforcement resource, the sheriff. The office was in Pine City, another 14 miles south of Hinckley. Maybe, she thought, that department might have a search and rescue team that could come to the campground to help look for the girls.

The usual trip to Hinckley from the campground took 25 minutes or less in a car. Alice knew the journey in the rain and in a 4-wheeler could take hours. Her plan was in peril after only five minutes. She met her first obstacle, a downed tree

across the road less than one-half mile from the ranger office. She stopped, got off the 4-wheeler and took her flashlight to get around the immense tree by walking down into the water-filled ditch to the right of the road. The water in the ditch was ankle deep. She figured she had nothing to lose and took the 4-wheeler into the ditch, avoiding the downed tree blocking the road. She plowed her way down the ditch until she was well past the large pine.

What she didn't think about was how she was going to get out of the ditch and back to the road. The slope was steep and would probably tip the 4-wheeler. There was no choice but to continue down the ditch. After a block, she came to a gravel road that crossed the ditch perpendicularly. She was trapped, or so she thought. Instead, off to her right looked like a ramp up to the gravel road. Alice gunned the engine, and the 4-wheeler climbed the so-called ramp and landed with a big bounce and thud on the dirt road. With the rain continuing to come down, she pushed her vehicle to the limit, using the gravel crossroad to bring her back to the main paved road. She was fortunate to have a piece of fiberglass as a roof over her vehicle. It shielded her to a degree from the torrent of rain still coming down.

The first tree trip down into the ditch routine was to be repeated three more times without issue. Alice was becoming confident that she was going to make it. Unfortunately, the fifth tree and ditch confrontation did not go well. As Ranger Alice drove into the ditch, the water was considerably deeper. The 4-wheeler immediately sank in the soft soil of the water-filled ditch. The tires were spinning but not moving the vehicle forward. Alice gunned it again, but to no avail. Now panic was setting in. She was stuck in the mud, miles from the campground, miles from Hinckley.

Alice got out of the 4-wheeler. The water was up over the wheels of her vehicle. Using the flashlight, she looked over the situation. There seemed to be no solution. She climbed back onto the 4-wheeler feeling defeated. The missing teens could be dead by the time she could walk to Hinckley. Sitting on the seat, feeling sorry for herself, she remembered a time when her dad's car was stuck in a snowbank. He had used a long metal pipe as a lever to help rock and release the car from the grip of the snow.   Alice figured it was worth a try and looked for a long branch or something she could use. Luckily, she found one that was long and still light enough for her to carry to the stuck vehicle. But the branch was only part of the hope. Next, she needed a rock that had some weight to it, but not too much. Alice guessed it would require about a six-inch diameter stone.

After walking a portion of the ditch with her flashlight, she found a rock on the other side of the ditch that she thought might work and required little digging to release it from its location. Alice took the rock and set it on the accelerator. The engine roared, and the tires spun, sending a huge spray of water behind the 4-wheeler. She backed the rock off the accelerator a bit to slow the spin of the wheels. Then she took the long branch behind the 4-wheeler and used it as a lever to inch the vehicle forward out of the grip of the mud. As soon as the vehicle gained some momentum, she dropped the branch and ran to the side of the vehicle and hopped on, kicking the rock off the accelerator, using her own foot to keep up the speed.

Three hours later, Alice pulled the 4-wheeler into a gas station that still had its lights on even at the late hour. She pulled her cell phone out, seeing a signal, she dialed 911. "911. What's your emergency? Sheriff Pine City," came the reply. Alice explained who she was, and that she was in Hinckley. She told him about all the downed trees, the lack of electricity, the tremendous damage, lack of ability to communicate, and the missing teenage girls.

At first, the sheriff said his department was overwhelmed dealing with tornado damage in his jurisdiction of over 1400 square miles. Not to be denied after her journey, the ranger said, "Yes, but you have communications, and electricity. I would imagine you have squad cars that aren't buried under fallen trees and you don't have several hundred campers trapped in a campground with only three rangers available. And besides, we're trying our best to search 53 square miles and two rivers for these teens."

The sheriff said he understood the urgency but didn't have the workforce to send to the campground to help. But he remembered he had a drone which had not been put into operation yet. He offered to bring it to the ranger and to meet Alice at the first roadblock by a downed tree on the route back to the campground.

The sheriff also indicated he would call the Pine County maintenance dept to get a front-end loader to clear a path for her 4-wheeler back to the ranger office. It would not be quick, since the vehicles were not known for their speed but rather the ability to lift heavy loads. Alice was grateful none-the-less. She didn't think she had the energy to deal with the water-filled ditches again.

By the time Alice hit the first tree roadblock, she could see the flashing lights and hear the siren from the sheriff's vehicle. Moments later, she had the drone and was awaiting the front loader. It arrived minutes later with an enormous claw dangling on the front arms of the large yellow machine. It took only moments for the loader to grab hold of the tree and pull it off to the side. The loader continued down the road towards the campground. It repeated what became a routine of pulling up to the tree, clamping on to it and pulling it off to the side of the road. By the time Ranger Alice pulled into the State Park, it was 4:30 am. Alice sweet-talked the front loader operator to pull two more trees to clear the campground road all the way to the Lodge. Rescue vehicles could now drive to the heart of the campground if needed.

Fifteen minutes earlier, Ranger Hugh Anderson had returned to the office from searching, with no success whatsoever, for the missing girls. He realized that the inability to talk with other rangers was hampering not only the search, but also individual ranger whereabouts. He did not know, for example, where his two other rangers were at the moment. Like Alice, hours earlier, he too headed to the maintenance shop. He remembered he had seen a portable generator a year ago when one of the maintenance shop guys was using it to build a new canoe rack. He was correct. It was in the corner of the roofless maintenance shop, but he did not know if was operable. Fortunately for Anderson, the generator was on wheels and moved fairly easily despite its significant weight. He wheeled it about a block to the ranger's office, hoping to use it to power up the radio and some lights.

Ranger Alice was thrilled to see a light on in the office as she pulled the 4-wheeler to the curb in front of the building. The generator motor was breaking the night's silence. Hugh, looking thoroughly exhausted, greeted Alice with a pointed question. "Where the heck have you been, Alice? I thought I told you your job tonight was to man the office here at the station." It was obvious Anderson was hot under the collar.

Alice was in no mood to let her boss give her grief at that moment. She summarized the night's various episodes, including her trip to Hinckley to get more help to look for the teens. She also showed him her new drone tool to help search the state park. It would be a multiple of times better than trying to cover the park on foot. The sheriff had told her the camera worked best when there was some daylight. Alice knew she had about thirty more minutes of darkness in which to practice flying the drone. She wanted to get it in the air at the first inkling of light in the new day. Time was of the essence for finding the lost teens. What Alice didn't know was now there were two additional teenagers who hadn't been heard from since the prior evening. Ranger Hugh looked at the woman with a drone in her hands and suddenly realized what his ranger had been through to get help. He turned and said, "I'm so sorry, Alice. You have my profound admiration. Let's get this thing in the air."

The forty-five minutes of drone flight time would never cover the whole state park property, so Alice was going to have to search what she considered potential areas where she thought the girls might be located. If the girls weren't located within those 45 minutes, the drone would have to be brought back to the ranger station and be charged by using the generator. Unfortunately, the sheriff told her it takes about 90 minutes to recharge the batteries, a real delay in the search.

Alice flew the drone down the entire paved path system since Ranger Hugh said he could not traverse the pathways with a 4-wheeler because of the trees across the path. He said they searched on foot all night, to no avail. Flying to the end of the pathways would at least give her a sign if there was any evidence of the girls. She would make the flight a quick one.

Like the McPherson boys, Alice felt the river would be about the only place to find the girls if they had any chance of being alive. Thus, it became the most important place to fly the drone. Twenty minutes of flight time had been used when she came upon, in the dim morning light, two bikes parked at the end of the paved trail. The owners of the bikes were nowhere to be found. Both bikes looked like boy's bikes and not the colorful girl's bikes that Mr. Edwards had described earlier. What the heck, she said to herself while hovering over the bikes. She knew the bikes had to be a recent addition to that spot, for they were both standing upright with their kickstands. No bike would have been upright throughout the tornado.

Twelve

Ranger Alice flew the drone in concentric circles around the bikes. Finally, she reached the riverbank and decided to burn up the remaining time, flying slowly over the bank. It was now light enough for the drone to provide good images of the riverbank. As she watched the drone monitor, she could not believe all the devastation. She began to think the search for life was fruitless. No one could have survived the storm.

Suddenly, the drone controller started beeping. Three minutes were left of the charge. The drone would have to be retrieved. But just as the ranger pressed the 'retrieve' button, a momentary glimpse of something reflective caught her eye. She flew the drone low and over the object. She realized it was a silver emergency survival blanket and that it had to have been put there after the tornado. At that instant, Patrick was awakened to the low whine of the drone and peered out from under the mylar tarp to wave at the drone. The drone rocked back and forth, showing the drone operator had seen Patrick.

Patrick then tore the mylar tarp off and woke up the others. He then had Katrina and Nate stand, but pointed to Elizabeth, who was wrapped in mylar and couldn't move. Patrick hoped the drone operator understood Elizabeth couldn't move on her own. Then, trying to show what was wrong with Elizabeth, he pointed at his own legs and made chopping motions. Again, the drone rocked back and forth, showing the operator understood. Then the drone flew off. Although the four weren't sure anything they conveyed to the drone was understood. Unknown to them, the drone operator immediately perceived perfectly the situation and the exact location.

Logistically, it would not be possible to help Elizabeth without a stretcher, ropes, and an entire team of people. The ranger realized they had no such equipment that could be easily moved to the rescue position miles from the ranger office. Then it came to her. They could ferry a stretcher basket and ropes down the river to that spot and slide Elizabeth and the basket down the slope into a canoe.

Unfortunately, it dawned on Ranger Alice the canoe storage rack was also in the tornado's path. There wasn't a canoe anywhere that hadn't been trashed. She needed another idea, something better. She used the ranger radio system, now powered by the generator, to see if the sheriff was monitoring her frequency as he promised. Indeed, he immediately responded by asking if the drone had found the girls. Alice reported in the affirmative, but they were miles down the river and on a precarious outcropping on the steep river bank. "I need a helicopter to drop a basket to recover one girl with possible broken legs."

"Let me see what I can do," said the sheriff. Ten minutes later, the sheriff called the ranger and told her he had secured a rescue helicopter out of the Twin Cities. It will be at the riverbank in another 20 minutes. The pilot will have two rescue team members in the copter to assist in the rescue.

Thirteen

Meanwhile, back on the slope of the riverbank, the four chatted about how long it was going to take for the rescuers to arrive. Both Nate and Patrick thought they would be coming on foot and would probably take several hours to get there with the equipment to move a person with broken legs. A helicopter never entered their minds. Thirty minutes later they heard the whooop, whooop, whooop of the blades and saw the copter overhead. They waved their silver mylar blankets and the copter's rotor wash almost blew the blankets out of their hands.

Over the helicopter loudspeaker, one of the rescue team said he was going to be dropped down to them, and then he would need everyone's help to get the girl with the broken legs into a basket that would be lowered from the copter. He told the four to cover their eyes to protect them from the debris in swirling winds created by the copter.

Moments later, a man in a jumpsuit and a helmet was on a cable to a place on the slope right above the four. He slid down the bank until he reached the location of the four teens. Introducing himself as Captain Ray Hanson, he proceeded to get scissors from his backpack and cut the mylar blanket off Elizabeth. He immediately noticed that her legs were splinted with branches and gauze wrap. "Ok, who's responsible for the branches and gauze?" asked Hanson.

Fearing they had done something terribly wrong, neither Patrick nor Nate responded to the helicopter crewman. They wondered if they were going to get yelled at. Could they have hurt Elizabeth instead by their actions? The brothers were on edge for what felt like an hour. In actuality, it was only seconds before Hanson, with a big smile on his face, said, "I'm really impressed with the quality of your first aid treatment for this young lady". Patrick & Nate gave each other a slight nod. The man from Rescue One was going to be ok in their eyes.

The Captain wanted help in rolling Elizabeth onto a blanket that had handles. It was going to take all of them to carefully lift Elizabeth into a rescue basket that was going to be lowered from the copter.

Once that was completed, along with some screams of pain from Elizabeth, Captain Hanson radioed for the copter basket. He again warned everyone of the coming nasty rotor wash from the copter blades, but they were going to have to endure it. The basket started dropping out of the sky. Hanson guided it through radio commands, caught it, and pulled it next to Elizabeth.

The four lifted the blanket containing Elizabeth into the basket. Elizabeth let out a scream, catching everyone off-guard. Hanson recovered quickly, promising everyone would try their best to not hurt her anymore. He covered Elizabeth with another covering before strapping her in. Then he gave the copter the 'up' sign. Basket and Elizabeth floated into the sky.

Once the basket had been secured into the helicopter, it immediately flew away from the river site. Hanson told the remaining three the copter would return for them after it took Elizabeth to the closest hospital in Sandstone, about 25 miles away. Hanson figured the group was starved and thirsty. He pulled out bottles of water and energy bars from his backpack. They surprised him, showing their empty water bottles and wrappers from the bars the boys had brought. However, none of the teens was above accepting a handout from Hanson.

The twenty-five-mile flight to the Sandstone hospital from the riverbank lasted less than fifteen minutes. The crew had radioed ahead, advising them to be ready to receive a teen with possible broken legs and shock. As the helicopter approached, the emergency room staff lined up on the mini tarmac. Minutes later, the Malibu teenager was loaded onto the shiny chrome gurney and rushed into the hospital emergency room.

The ER doctor took one look at Elizabeth's legs with the branches wrapped with gauze around her legs and asked Elizabeth, "who splinted your legs like this young lady? I think they might have saved you a lot of agony." Before she answered, the doctor continued, "Let's get this gauze cut off and branches removed and get you to Xray."

Fourteen

The helicopter returned and hovered overhead. Again, the blade wash created a mini wind storm with dust and small bits of debris flying through the air, forcing those on the ground to squint. A cable with two harnesses started to descend from the copter down towards the waiting teens and captain. A crewman standing in an open door was waving and simultaneously directing the cable. Suddenly, there was a large bang. It almost sounded like a rifle blast. Smoke started pouring out of the helicopter engine. The copter swayed. It twisted and turned, obviously out of control. No longer was it going to be the rescue vehicle they had expected. It was spinning its way to earth. The copter was going to crash onto the bank where the four were located. Captain Hanson yelled at the top of his lungs, "Run to the top of the bank!" No one hesitated. The four grabbed branches from fallen trees to aid in climbing the steep bank. The noise of the out-of-control copter was deafening.

Seconds passed, but it seemed like minutes, as the copter fell from the sky. Somehow, some way, the pilot at the last second was able to divert the copter away from the four on the riverbank and instead plunge it into the river. It landed on its side. Water sprayed everywhere. The sound of the blades hitting the water and the mud of the river bottom was ear shattering.

Hanson changed direction the moment he saw the copter head towards the water. He was now on the move down the steep bank towards the river and the quickly sinking copter with its two occupants. Patrick and Nate were less than a step behind. As the three hit the river's edge, they all jumped in and swam towards the huge rotor blades of the copter still protruding from the iron color of the fast-moving river.

It was no small challenge. The current from the recent rains was strong, pushing the swimmers away from the copter. Thankfully, the copter maintained its position because several of the individual blades had become buried in the mud of the river bottom. Nate and Patrick were both strong swimmers, having started lessons when they were toddlers. Hanson reached the copter first. He yelled, "I'll go to the front. You guys check out the back of the copter." He dove under in the dark river water to find his team members. Nate and Patrick followed him down.

They saw Hanson's feet as he swam through the open door to the front of the copter and the body of the pilot still strapped into his seat. He began frantically working to get the unconscious pilot out of his harness. The boys swam into the cargo area, trying to find the man who had, moments earlier, been preparing the cable to bring the teens off the steep river embankment. They located him crumpled in a corner of the hold of the copter. He was tangled in the rescue cable.

Their lungs felt like they were going to explode. Quickly, they untangled what they could and dragged the helmeted copter team member to the door. Together, Nate and Patrick pulled the unconscious man out of the copter and to the surface. Hanson appeared a moment later, himself gasping for air. He had the pilot in his grasp.

Hanson shouted, "We've got to get them to the shore for CPR and fast!" The boys each grasped the unmoving arms of the crewman, who, only a short time earlier, had lifted Elizabeth to the copter. Swimming, pulling, gasping, the boys fought the current, dragging the lifeless body. Captain Hanson was himself struggling in the water with the unconscious pilot. All he could think about at that moment was to get the body of his friend and teammate through the rapidly moving river current to the riverbank.

Completely exhausted, Nate took off the co-pilot's helmet and Patrick immediately began chest compressions. Per what Grandpa Al had taught them, Nate cleared the man's passageway. Hanson was doing the same with the pilot.

As the boys worked on the crewman, Captain Hanson was yelling, "Come on, come on, Jake!"

Katrina, having slid down the bank, was standing next to Patrick and Nate doing CPR, asked "What can I do to help?"

Patrick looked up at her and said, "Go see if you can give Captain Hanson help with doing chest compressions on the pilot."

About that same instant, there was noise and a noticeable gasp of air from the helicopter cable operator, Mike Peterson. He was alive. Meanwhile, Hanson continued CPR on the pilot and yelled, "We need the AED. It's in the copter."

Patrick asked in a loud voice as he was ready to jump back into the water, "where?"

"It's on the wall in a bracket behind the pilot's seat." The moments were passing. It didn't look good for the pilot. Neither of the boys had ever had anyone die in front of them.

"I'm going for it," yelled Patrick, diving into the river. Nate watched his brother fight the current as he swam towards the mostly submerged helicopter with only a few of the blades sticking up out of the river at a weird angle. Moments later, he disappeared under the bronze-colored river water. Searching the darkened interior, Patrick put his hands on the wall behind the pilot's seat and found the AED in a bracket. Popping it loose from its mounting, he headed out of what felt like a tomb.

Katrina was helping the cable operator, Mike, sit up. Nate went to the river to help his brother, jumping into the water as soon as he saw Patrick break the surface. He swam as fast as he could to retrieve the AED from Patrick, bringing it to shore and the hands of Captain Hanson, who had not stopped compressions. The captain quickly ripped the pilot's shirt open and attached the leads. Yelling, "clear!" he pushed the AED button as it delivered an electronic shock to the pilot. Nothing. The body jumped from the shock but continued to be lifeless.

Hanson hit the button again. Another electrical shock. Suddenly Hanson yelled, "Heartbeat! We've got him back!" Jake began breathing on his own, but was still unconscious.

Katrina, with excitement in her voice, screamed only one word at the top of her lungs, "Yes!"

Hanson turned to Nate and Patrick. "You guys are something else. Thank you for now helping me save my team."

"What are we going to do now?" asked Katrina.

The response came from Mike, the now half-way alert co-pilot and cable operator, "We sit and wait. I heard Jake radio a 'Mayday' on our way down into the water. I'm sure a search helo will be in the air by now. Hopefully, they'll have plotted our location from that last transmission and be here soon."

Hanson checked out the pilot's injuries. Looks like Jake might have a broken arm and probably a concussion from the looks of the bruise on his forehead. I'm guessing internal injuries too from the bruises on his chest. He then turned to the cable operator and said, "Mikey, how ya doing, man? It's good to see you in one piece."

"I'm banged up pretty bad from that less than soft landing, but I can move all my appendages. I sure don't know what happened. One minute the bird is moving in to lift you guys out of here and the next, well, you know what happened next. It was almost like the engine exploded. It was that quick. Thank you, kids. We owe you our lives!"

73

Fifteen

Ranger Alice had tracked down Katrina's parents and the McPhersons to be at the ranger station for the landing of the rescue copter. She explained to both sets of parents that she had found their children with the use of the drone and that they were all alive. She explained the boys had showed through a chopping motion that one girl might have broken legs. The ranger then told about her conversation with the sheriff and his call to the Twin Cities for a rescue copter. Alice described what she remembered from the drone pictures of the girl with the possible broken legs. Instantly, the Edwards knew it was Elizabeth and not their daughter, although that discovery did little to relieve their anxiousness.

The small group watched from the parking lot of the ranger station, the first copter fly overhead towards the Sandstone hospital. Accordingly, they knew the flight was for Elizabeth with possible broken legs. They also watched as the copter flew overhead on the return from the hospital towards the river.

Unfortunately, they also heard an explosion type noise even though they were miles from the site. The silence that followed the crash was unnerving. They assumed what they heard was the crash of the copter. When the whoop, whoop, whoop sound of the blades hitting the air didn't return, fear entered the adults standing at the ranger station. It was too quiet. No helicopter. They had no idea of what had happened at the river to their children and the bird that was to bring their loved ones to the ranger station landing area.

Alice couldn't take it any longer. She knew the pressure that the parents were experiencing. No one standing there had any idea how to contact the helicopter, but she remembered it was the sheriff who called the helicopter base in the Twin Cities. She left the group and went into the ranger office. She radioed him, explaining the situation. He promised to call the base as soon as they disconnected. Moments later, the radio crackled back to life. It was the sheriff reporting in. The helicopter base reported they had received a mayday message from Rescue One. They had lost contact with the team. They were sending Rescue Two immediately to the last place of radio contact with Rescue One.

The ranger now did not know what to do with the information. Were the kids on board? Did anyone survive? What happened? Will the parents worry even more if they now know the copter went down? She finally decided the best thing was to tell the parents what she knew from the sheriff.

As soon as Ranger Alice exited the building, she sensed all eyes were on her. She could feel the tension in the lives of the parents as they wondered what news she had carried with her from the sheriff. Alice told the parents what she had learned from the call with the sheriff. Ella Edwards broke down in sobs. Her husband, Bob, immediately clutched her and hugged her in a tight embrace. He was silent.

Grandpa Al wondered if he had done the right thing by encouraging the boys to look for the girls. He thought of the training, the self-sufficiency of the grandsons, but knew none of it would matter if there was an explosion aboard the copter.

Jay McPherson bent over. He couldn't even fathom something happening to his boys. What would he tell his wife, Carole? The unknown and the wait became excruciating.

Sixteen

Whoop, whoop, whoop. Still miles away, the battered group of teens and half-alive helicopter crewmen heard the familiar sound of a helicopter that would within a minute hover over them on the edge of the river. The loudspeaker from the copter again blared, "Everyone ok? I'm dropping a radio down on the cable."

Katrina was the first to grab the cable and secure the radio, bringing it over to Hanson. He reported to the crew in the bird that Jake needed to get emergency care ASAP, breathing but unconscious. First priority. No idea of the extent of internal injuries. They needed the rescue basket.

Like the earlier process with Elizabeth, the crew dropped the basket, dangling it from the cable. Hanson secured it next to pilot Jake. Together, Katrina, Patrick, Nate, and Hanson were able to lift the seemingly lifeless body and secure him into the basket. Less than two minutes later, the crew in the copter had the basket in the cargo area and was heading off full speed to the Sandstone hospital. The crew radioed Hanson, telling him they would be back to pick him and the others up in a half hour.

Once inside the copter, the EMT on board administered oxygen to Jake and monitored his vitals. The co-pilot was on the radio to the base station in the Twin Cities. "Rescue One is down in the St. Croix River. Pilot Jake is in our bird, unconscious but breathing on his own. On our way to Sandstone Emergency Room. Rescue One's two other members, Ray, and Mike, are both at the river's edge with three teens, two boys and a girl. All appear to be safe. Will return to pick them up after the hospital run. Please communicate with the sheriff."

The parents, Grandpa Al, and Ranger Alice watched as the second helicopter passed over the State Park obviously heading in the same direction as the first. They knew it was another hospital flight. As the copter disappeared from sight, so too did the distinctive noise of the blades pounding the air. Ranger Alice's radio crackled to life once again. It was the sheriff. Knowing all would hear the transmission, Alice hesitated, then said, "Go Ahead, Sheriff."

"I have good news and bad news. First, the bad news. The copter named Rescue One, with two crew members aboard, crashed into the river after returning from bringing a teenage girl to the Sandstone Hospital for possible broken legs. From what I understand, upon the return to the river just as the copter was to rescue the three teens and a member of the crew, there was some kind of explosion, and the copter crashed into the river. The pilot and co-pilot have been rescued. The pilot, however, breathing on his own is unconscious. A second copter named Rescue Two is flying him to the Sandstone hospital at this very moment.

"Here's the good news. Rescue Two will return to the riverbank after the Sandstone Hospital to pick up the three young people and two crew members from Rescue One. I'm happy to report, they all are fine. They should be arriving at the ranger station in about 30 to 45 minutes."

Immediately, the mood changed within the small group gathered outside the ranger station. From the depths of despair and worry to cautious exuberance. They hugged each other, but silently wondered if the return trip from the hospital would meet the same fate as Rescue One.

Per plan, Rescue Two made a return flight to the river and the copter crash site. The two pilots and the three teens joyfully received the now familiar pattern of a hovering copter and long dangling cable. After confirming Patterson could handle being lifted into the copter via harness, Hanson assisted his team member to get attached to the cable and watched him being lifted skyward.

The cable was returned to the earth, the second time with two harnesses. Captain Hanson said, "Katrina, you and I get to go before the boys. Then I'll return to pull up one of them."

Hanson climbed into one harness and handed the other to Katrina. He told her he was going to clip her harness to his and that together they would hold on to the cable and be lifted to the copter. He also suggested that she might want to look outward instead of down as they were being lifted. Kiddingly, he added, "This might be a once in a lifetime uplifting experience."

"Captain, would you mind if Nate and I harness up ourselves? And second, would it be okay if you didn't pull us into the copter, but instead flew us back to the campground while dangling from the cable?" said Patrick.

"Well, I can't say it would be protocol from a safety standpoint, but I can't think of a better way for you to experience a bird's-eye view of the park. I'll confirm it's okay with the crew when Katrina and I are up there and secure. If I don't come back down, you know I was successful in talking the crew into letting you fly on the cable."

After Hanson and Katrina were on their way to the helo overhead, Patrick turned to his brother and said, "You up for this, bro? It could be a ride of a lifetime."

"Can't wait," said the younger. "Imagine what dad is going to say when he sees us dangling from a helicopter cable."

"Ya, I just hope he doesn't have a heart attack," replied Patrick. "You know that blast we heard before the copter started blowing smoke? Didn't it sound like a rifle shot, like when we practiced on Gramp's farm?"

Nate didn't answer his brother. At that moment, the cable with two harnesses dropped from the sky. Secured to the cable and to each other, the helo lifted them skyward. It was a flight they would remember for the rest of their lives. Dangling, moving across the sky at 40 mph, feeling the force of the wind in their faces and the ability to see for miles created a mind-blowing experience. The full force of the tornado's power became even more clear as they viewed and experienced the flight over the state park. "Can you believe what the tornado did to this beautiful place?" yelled Nate to his bro. "It seems almost impossible."

Patrick didn't have a chance to answer. Both cable fliers spotted the ranger station and a group of happy-looking adults. A female ranger was pointing at them. Grandpa Al had a big smile on his face. Dad looked more worried than happy. He had been up all-night wondering what and where his boys were in the tornado-made mess. Moments later, the copter lowered the two teens to the ground. Then, as they removed their harnesses, the cable was hydraulically lifted back into the copter.

Shortly thereafter, the bird was on the ground with an eager female teen quickly exiting and running into the arms of her parents. All three teens were being hugged. The veil of darkness was lifting. The copter's engine was shut down and the five adults in jump suits exited as well. After the hugs all around, Captain Hanson told the Edwards family his team would count it a privilege to fly them to the Sandstone hospital to see Elizabeth, the young lady with the possible broken legs.

Prior to the copter take off, the rescue team relayed to the parents and Grandpa Al what they had found on the slope. The mylar survival blankets, the splints on the legs of Elizabeth, the water, and energy bars. Grandpa Al smiled. Captain Hanson continued, "I still don't know how these two boys had the ability to not only find the girls in the dark, but also take such good care of them. After I saw the size of the log that was on top of Elizabeth's legs, well, let's just say these three teens performed admirably, together lifting the log and pulling Elizabeth free.

He continued saying, "I was on the slope with the teens when we watched Rescue One go down with both Jake and Mike inside. Patrick, Nate and I were able to swim, find them, and bring them both to shore, whereupon the boys gave CPR to Mike while I worked on Jake. My teammates owe their lives to those young men."

Katrina piped up with a smile, "And don't forget, these two guys brought us energy bars for supper. We were starving."

The entire story of the rescues would have to wait to be re-told. Moments later the blades were again whirling, and the bird was in the sky heading at 100 mph to the Sandstone Hospital.

Patrick was the first to say, "Hey, what's for breakfast? I could use a big stack of pancakes, a slab of bacon, and a half gallon of orange juice."

Grandpa Al piped up, "Is that all? Well, boys, you're going to have to work for your breakfast. Your dad and I have been so busy with the search and helping other campers all night long we haven't had a chance to upright the tent trailer or set up anything. We haven't even had a chance to take an inventory of what's damaged or what can be saved. Let's see if we can't get the tent trailer turned over as a start."

But it was going to take more than the four to upright the tent trailer. As if on cue, eight other campers showed up just like magic as the McPhersons were trying to turn over the camper. It was no problem at all with the additional manpower. Nate figured it was a good thing that their pickup was still right side up, otherwise the juice and milk would have coated the interior of the truck.

Ranger Alice drove up in her trusty 4-wheeler and introduced herself. She wanted to talk with the two young men who not only found the girls but also saved a man's life with CPR. She said the boys were a true inspiration to the entire campground. The ranger announced she had seen their bikes at the end of the trail with the drone and had convinced the helicopter team to make one more quick flight once they were done flying the Edwards to Sandstone Hospital. The copter team will attach the cable to your bikes and fly them here to the lodge. Just as Ranger Alice finished telling the McPhersons about the bikes, the boys heard the familiar whooop, whooop of the copter blades. Their bikes were now dangling from the same long cable that had held them. Alice told the boys to run over to the lodge area to unhook their bikes as the copter hovered.

Both Nate and Patrick ran and felt again the now familiar strong rotor wind wash from the copter. The loudspeaker squealed. It was Captain Hanson. "Gentlemen, you have our profound respect. Anytime you want to fly with us, you let us know." Hanson leaned out the open door of the copter and saluted the boys. After the guys unhooked their bikes from the cable, they mouthed a 'thank you' to Captain Hanson. A moment later, the copter was flying at over 100 mph back to its base in the Twin Cities.

Ranger Alice updated the four McPhersons with the news about the front-end loader clearing the trees off the road between the campground and Hinckley. She neglected to mention the part about her brave, middle of the night excursion on the 4-wheeler to get help and the drone. "We don't have electricity yet, but with the generator supplying power to run a few lights and our radios, we can at least communicate with the outside world. And now we also have access in and out of the campground."

Seventeen

While Elizabeth was getting her X-rays, Mr. and Mrs. Edwards and Katrina arrived at the hospital with the compliments of the helicopter team. The ER staff updated them and moved them down the hall to await the return of Elizabeth from radiology.

Thirty minutes later, Elizabeth was rolled into the room on a gurney. The radiologist and ER doctor were right behind. They introduced themselves to the Edwards with the doctor taking the lead, saying, "It's too bad Elizabeth isn't older. She should go out and buy a lottery ticket. The X-rays revealed she is a very lucky young woman. Her left leg has been badly bruised, but surprisingly, it is not broken. However, the right leg tibia showed a small crack, but on review we don't think it's anything to worry about. That leg, as well, is certainly severely bruised. We're going to recommend splints on both legs, to keep Elizabeth comfortable, but no more branches and gauze," smiled the doctor.

Then, turning to Elizabeth, he continued, "We'll send you home with a set of crutches to enable you to stay off those legs for a few days. Give us some time to get you splinted up, and the crutches customized for you, and then you'll be ready to go."

"Ahhh, Doc, do you have Uber in Sandstone? We all arrived by helicopter," said Mrs. Edwards.

"Afraid not, but we have the next best thing. We have a taxi service. I'll have the desk call for you and set it up. The service uses mini-vans, so it should be easy to get Elizabeth up into the vehicle."

Even though the doctor made it sound like Elizabeth would be ready to go in a short time, it took a number of hours before she was released. Other emergencies took precedence, and Elizabeth was relegated to lying on a hospital bed awaiting splints and crutches. She was moved to a curtained off area of the ER where the Edwards could wait with her and keep her company. The hospital provided folding chairs for the family to sit with her while they waited.

"Who would have thought you young ladies would spend your time in Minnesota in a tornado, a night on a riverbank and a day in a small-town community hospital... and oh, did I leave out that helicopter ride? Elizabeth, I'll bet you're never ever going to want to camp with us again," laughed Mr. Edwards.

Eighteen

The boys were famished after the long night and early morning helicopter rescue. Once the camper was upright, the four McPhersons set about to make breakfast. The pickup truck tailgate served as the table and the food prep counter, since picnic tables were basically non-existent after the storm. After pancakes, bacon, and a gallon of orange juice for breakfast, the four realized how exhausted they were.

Gramps suggested they grab 40 winks. "What the heck are 40 winks?" asked Nate.

"Ahhh, I forgot at the moment that you guys aren't Shakespear followers yet. The 40 winks expression has been around a long time. Supposedly, Shakespear first used it in the early 1600s and it's been with us ever since. Yah, I know that was a lot more info than you asked for. It simply means a short sleep. You guys up for that?"

The tent trailer wasn't the easiest place for Nate and Patrick because the two adults each had their own bed at either end of the tent trailer. The boys had to sleep on a convertible space in the middle of the camper. Put away the dining table, throw on some cushions and the center space became a bed large enough for two sleeping bags and the occupants. Both Nate and Patrick were happy to strip down to their skivvies before climbing into their sleeping bag. Their clothes were a muddy mess. As Nate climbed out of his pants, the coin fell out and rolled across the vinyl flooring of the tent trailer.

"Hey, keep your mitts off that, Patrick. That's my silver dollar. Finders' keepers," said Nate, following the rolling coin. Gramps and dad simply groaned, not even having enough interest to look at what Nate was talking about.

While the McPhersons were catching their 40 winks, the ranger station was a beehive of activity. Through the use of the generator and communications with the sheriff, the emergency management department of the State had ordered a COW to be delivered to the tornado damaged areas, including the state park. A COW was a portable 'cell on wheels' specifically designed for quick deployment where cell service was needed. The COW was to arrive from the Twin Cities to the ranger station about 9:30 am and be functional shortly thereafter.

About a half-hour into the 40 winks, Jay's cell phone started ringing. Groggily, he reached and fumbled around for the phone. Finally, bringing it up to his ear, he whispered, "Hello".

"Jay, are you all right? asked Carole. How are the boys and your dad? We're seeing drone coverage of the tornado on the news here. It looks awful."

"Hon, we're all fine. I'm whispering because we've been up all night and are just trying to sleep a little. You'd be proud of your boys. They helped find and rescue a couple of kids lost in yesterday's tornado. By the way, how did you call me? We haven't had any kind of cell service. Let everyone know we're fine. We're going to stick around for a while and help out around here. And now that we have cell service, we'll call you later today and give you a full update."

"Sounds good. I was so worried when I saw the news and all the damage. Bye dear."

"Bye, love you. Thanks for checking up on us," said Jay.

Although the camper was silent for another three hours as the McPherson's caught something over 40 winks. They were awakened by a truck rumbling past the tent trailer. Jay unzipped the canvas window. The noise was from a large tow truck on its way to a nearby campsite, where a tree sat atop a Chevrolet Suburban. The noise awoke the other three as well.

"I don't think I like the idea of 40 winks. I could use another eight hours instead," said Patrick as he tried to move his tired body off the modified bed.

"We've obviously been discovered by the rest of the world. I'll bet we'll see a lot of tow trucks, front-end loaders, loggers and storm chasers come through here in the coming hours," said Jay. "Mom called while you were sleeping. She said we made the news. Drone pictures of the tornado path were being shown. She said it looked bad. I guess we can confirm that. While we were laying here, they must have set up a COW for cell service."

"What the heck are you talking about, dad? Since when do cows have anything to do with cell phone service?" asked Nathan.

Gramps stepped into the conversation, answering, "COW is the abbreviation for 'cell on wheels' or, in other words, a portable cell phone tower that basically can be trucked anywhere there's a road. They're used in all kinds of disasters until they can get the regular cell towers back into operation. What do you say we take a hike around to see what has been happening in the campground for the last few hours?

I'm certain there's a lot of activity now with cell phone service. We can start at our logging camping area and eventually end up walking through the section where all the RV's are. Somewhere along the way, I'm sure we'll find the COW.

Nineteen

The trip around the campground was not pretty. They found other tent trailers that had been set up prior to the tornado, in shreds. They counted over 30 enormous trees blown down just within the tent camping areas. There wasn't a tent in sight. There were dozens of campers picking through the debris, trying to find anything salvageable of their belongings. Some were attempting to make their cars drivable. Most of the vehicles, if they weren't totally destroyed, had the windows blown out. Although there was a general sadness among the campers because of the loss of all their belongings, everyone stopped what they were doing to talk with the McPherson clan and, particularly the two teens, to thank them for their bravery. Word had spread throughout the campground of the rescues and the part the boys had played in them. Everywhere they looked, people were using their cell phones. One conversation after another focused on asking relatives to provide help in getting campers back home.

As they walked towards the other parts of the State Park, they saw the lodge where they had taken shelter from the tornado. It was still standing, but it was missing a portion of the roof. Gramps silently thanked the builders from so many years ago that had used their skills to build the sturdy structure. It had saved not only their lives but also all who were in the campground when the tornado struck.

Continuing towards the ranger station, they saw the COW. It looked like a large, oversized tent trailer, about nine or ten feet tall, with a trailer hitch sticking out the front end of it. On top there was a communications disk of some type and a pole, maybe thirty feet tall, in the air. It had a large wire that twisted around it all the way to the top. Another antenna was located on the very top of the pole. Pretty cool.

"Maybe we can find Ranger Alice and thank her for going all the way to Hinckley on the 4-wheeler. She is really a hero. By herself, she contacted law enforcement, secured the drone that found you guys and got a front-end loader here in the middle of the night to clear the road. Bringing this COW here wouldn't have been possible without her bravery," said Jay.

It was late in the afternoon by the time the McPherson's tour of the campground led them to the RV portion of the state park. This segment, unlike other areas of the campground, accommodated RV rigs. It had water and electric hookups at every site. The sanitary dump station was nearby as well. Although this section of the park did not have as many trees as the tent section, it was almost made barren by the tornado. The smaller, lighter RVs suffered the most damage, but not even the most expensive large units were immune from the wrath of the storm.

It was a repeat performance as the boys were constantly being hailed by the adults, wanting to know about the night on the riverbank. When they came around the loop, they spotted the Edward's large trailer and what used to be their new Chevy Crew cab pickup. Katrina and Elizabeth had told the boys about the big rigs last night as they talked under the mylar survival tarp. However, seeing it for the first time, in person, it was larger than they could have ever imagined.

One of the smaller RVs laying on its side was being attended to by another tow truck. The workers were attaching a cable to pull it into an upright position. The owners and a crowd of concerned bystanders were watching.

When the four approached the Edward's site, they found the family sitting together around a campfire. Elizabeth was with them, crutches laying by the side of her cloth camping chair. Katrina ran to meet the McPhersons as soon as she saw them round the bend on the loop of sites 42-55. First, she said hello to Grandpa Al and Jay, telling them how thankful she was for Patrick and Nathan. Then she invited the four, "Won't you please come and meet my parents and Elizabeth? She's back from the hospital." Patrick and Nate had a hard time believing this was the same Katrina, now in clean clothes and dry hair. Neither would comment, but both were impressed with the new look.

The $100,000 RV, Mr. Edward's pride and joy, stood tall, but bore the scars of severe dents and shattered windows. Every surface looked like someone took a hammer to it.

Elizabeth yelled, "Nate and Patrick... come here. Mr. and Mrs. Edwards, these are the guys who splinted my legs and who found us on the riverbank."

"Yes Elizabeth, we've already met them at the ranger station. In all the action at the hospital, we neglected to tell you the rest of the rescue story. Maybe the McPhersons will sit down with us for a few minutes and the boys can tell you what happened after you were airlifted to the hospital," said Bob, Katrina's dad.

Elizabeth, like Katrina, had obviously showered and had changed into a cute top and shorts. She was glowing, with her hair dropping gracefully over her shoulders. Her plastic splinted legs extended outward from the camping chair to a small end table in front of her. The undamaged table had evidently been in the RV during the storm. They sat together around the campfire. Katrina's mother, Ella, brought out lemonades to the group. The parents couldn't thank the boys enough for finding the girls and for taking such good care of them.

Elizabeth, however, wondered what had happened while she was in the hospital. "Well, fess up guys, what did I miss out on while I was visiting Mr. ER Doc?"

Patrick looked at Nate and laughed. "Well, you didn't miss much, I guess. Just a helicopter crash, some CPR, a river dive for an AED and a ride over the park while dangling from a helicopter cable. Did I cover the highlights, bro?"

Katrina jumped in and said, "Wait a minute, you missed the part about running for our lives when we thought the copter was going to crash on top of us."

"Yup, and I thought there was enough excitement living through a tornado and being found in the dead of night by a couple of guys. And of course, it was pretty cool to ride in a basket up to a hovering helicopter," laughed the girl with the crutches.

"Elizabeth, did you see a copter pilot who was brought into the ER while you were there?" asked Patrick. "His name is Jake. He was unconscious and had possible internal injuries. I sure hope he's okay."

"No, I didn't see him, but the ER staff made me wait a long time to get checked out because they were working with other emergencies. Jake might have been one of them. Sorry I knew nothing about the crash, otherwise I would have asked," said Elizabeth. "Oh, by the way, the ER doc liked the splint work that you guys did with the branches and the gauze. He thought I might like his plastic version better, however."

The parents had a good laugh at Elizabeth's splint report and then circled around to the question of what their families were going to do next. The entire area was still without electricity, but thanks to the COW, there was cell phone service. Loved ones now could be alerted, and those who had disabled vehicles could make arrangements for rides back home.

Bob was the first to answer the question. "You know, I drove into this campground a few days ago with a brand-new pickup truck and a beautiful new RV. They were my pride and joy. Now look at them. They look like they've been through a war and are hardly recognizable from the way they looked when we left California. And do you know what? I don't even care.

"Over these past 24 hours, I've been taught something I needed to learn. This experience has reminded that prized possessions, the things that we think are pretty cool, are absolutely nothing compared to the lives of our loved ones. My values have been more than misaligned. They were really screwed up.

"I haven't talked it over with my family yet, but I want to propose we stick around here for at least a few days to help around the campground. It looks like there are a lot of folks who could use some help to put their lives and their belongings back together. I'll bet the rangers can find some things that they need help with around here as well."

Jay, who was usually rather reserved, said, "I couldn't agree with you more. It only takes a night like we've just experienced to be reminded of how precious our kids are to us. We haven't had time to talk about our plans yet either, but it seems to me your idea of lending a hand with cleanup around here would be a good thing."

Elizabeth became sullen as she realized everyone around the campfire could easily move around. Not so much for her. She could use the crutches, but it would be slow going. She wondered what she would do while everyone else was helping others.

Nate, sensing Elizabeth's lack of mobility, said, "Hey Liz, since you're sort of a celebrity, maybe you could talk Ranger Alice into letting you scoot around the campground in her 4-wheeler. You could bring people whatever they need."

"Hey that sounds like fun. I've never driven a 4-wheeler before. Do you think the ranger will let me?" asked Elizabeth.

"Maybe we're getting ahead of ourselves," said Ella, Katrina's mom. "Did you ever think that we might actually be asked to leave the park as soon as possible? Almost every aspect of the campground is damaged and beyond the repair skills of most of us. For example, just think of clearing all the trees. It's going to take a lot of heavy equipment. And how about the missing roofs? I think we'd better be prepared to think all of us as visitors are going to be asked to clear out so the professionals can do the work."

At that very moment, the group heard the familiar sound of a 4-wheeler bouncing along on the gravel road. The ranger was using a loudspeaker, "All camper meeting at 6 pm at the lodge building. Everyone encouraged to be in attendance."

As the 4-wheeler past the Edward's campsite, they realized the ranger making the announcement was Hugh Anderson. He stopped his vehicle as soon as he saw the teens and walked over towards the group.

"Ranger Anderson, how are you doing? It's been quite the 24 hours," said Bob Edwards.

"Hello all, I'm sorry I haven't had time to stop by and meet the young people who were able to survive a tornado in what used to be a forest. And I understand you young men were the ones that somehow found the girls and also provided help in saving a couple of helicopter crew members," said Anderson.

Patrick couldn't get the pilot, Jake, out of his head. He blurted out, "Have you heard anything about the copter pilot, Jake, who was taken to the hospital?"

"Actually, just as I was leaving the office, I was informed that Jake is now conscious. He's pretty banged up and being kept at the hospital overnight. His buddies on Rescue Two are going to fly up from the cities tomorrow to check him out of the hospital and fly him back to North Memorial, a trauma hospital in Minneapolis. I understand he'll spend the next couple weeks there before heading home," said the ranger.

"Wow, he's going to be okay! It hardly seems possible. He looked awful when he was lifted off that riverbank," responded Nate.

"Yes," said Ranger Anderson, "We have a lot to be thankful for. Hey Elizabeth, you don't have to use the crutches to get to the meeting. I'll be back with the 4-wheeler to pick you up." As he finished the sentence, he turned the key, and his 4-wheeler came to life. A moment later, he was back on the gravel road, continuing to spread the news about the camper meeting in less than an hour.

"Well, any bets on what is going to be said at the meeting?" said Ella. "My guess is that we're going to find out the park is going to be closed up and we'll all be asked to leave."

Twenty

Sitting around the campfire, the reality set in. The McPhersons and the Edwards family, plus Elizabeth, were very different. Each of the adults tried to think of things to talk about. It was reminiscent of the first few hours on the bank of the river for the teens.

Mr. Edwards, Bob, when asked about what he did for a living, told the group he was a hedge fund manager and was a multi-millionaire. The revelation didn't go over too well with the McPhersons or, for that matter, with Ella and Katrina, who realized how 'braggy' it sounded.

When it came time for Jay McPherson to tell about his occupation simply said, "I plant grass seed for a living." Patrick and Nate groaned. In reality, their dad owned a large, well-known landscape company in Minneapolis.

Grandpa Al never let on that he was a retired agent, having spent a lot of time training his grandsons. Around the campfire that afternoon, he was a hobby farmer. The adults were struggling to find some common things that they both shared that would make their conversation easier. They hit on comparing Malibu's to Golden Valley's weather.

Once they had exhausted that topic, Grandpa Al asked the Edwards what brought them to St. Croix State Park. The retired agent was a master at reading people and giving them a perfect lead to a better conversation topic.

Bob picked up the ball and ran with it. He told about having the money to purchase both the new RV and the pickup truck and how they had planned based on Ella finding the magazine advertisements about Minnesota state parks, the lakes, and the forests. "So," he said, "here we are. I came here so proud of my purchase of the equipment."

The teens tried to be polite and listen, but they about lost all interest when they thought Bob was starting in on money talk. However, he took everyone back to something he had mentioned earlier, "Did you know money is absolutely meaningless when you have a daughter and her best friend missing?"

Ella relived the past 24 hours, and a tear trickled down her cheek. The thought of never seeing her daughter again had been overwhelming. "And thanks to you guys, we have our girls back. We will forever remember your act of courage."

The boys began to blush. They didn't know what to do or say. Grandpa Al again stepped in. "I think we can all celebrate tonight. The entire campground of over 200 people are alive and unhurt. It's honestly almost a miracle considering the strength of the tornado. I think the past twenty-four hours have taught all of us to re-examine what we value."

Ranger Hugh's promised return to pick up Elizabeth to bring her to the lodge meeting interrupted the adult conversation. Bob and Ella helped Elizabeth up onto the bench seat of the 4-wheeler. Unfortunately, it wasn't without some sharp moans of pain. Moments later, Ranger Anderson pointed the machine toward the lodge, driving slowly to avoid jostling his passenger.

A crowd immediately surrounded Elizabeth when she arrived at the lodge. Everyone there knew the story of the teen's legs being splinted by the boys, the helicopter ride, and the hospital visit. She was barraged with questions.

When Katrina and the boys walked into the building, the whole place broke out in a spontaneous, loud cheer. Everyone was clapping. About 26 hours earlier, a couple hundred campers were not clapping and cheering but huddled together in fear in the same building. Now less than 60 campers were left, the others had left either on their own or by help from friends or relative's vehicles.

When the clapping and cheering stopped, it became clear, like the day before, there was plenty of wondering in the room. The big question was, what was going to happen next?

Twenty-one

At three minutes after 6:00 pm, ranger Hugh Anderson stepped up to the front of the room and with an authoritative sounding voice said, "I'd like to thank all of you for your patience in this extremely difficult situation. Tonight, I want to both update you with what we know about the impact of the tornado and also what will happen here at St. Croix State Park, beginning tomorrow.

"First, I want to introduce to you a very special person. Last night, with the rain pouring down and the wind blowing like crazy, she found a working ranger 4-wheeler and on her own drove the 4-wheeler all the way to Hinckley. This was despite roads being impassable and not having any communications here.

She was determined to get cell service to notify the sheriff of the missing two girls and the plight of the campground after the tornado. Our hero among the rangers tonight, Ranger Alice Harrison."

After a long, standing ovation by the campers, everyone became silent and Ranger Hugh resumed, "And now let me introduce four people who I see are already known campground wide. First, the two teens who can go home and brag that they survived a tornado while being outside in an unprotected area, Elizabeth and Katrina. Young ladies, we are so thankful that you are alive and safe here tonight."

Again, the room erupted with loud cheers and another long, standing ovation. Tears were streaming down the faces of Katrina's parents. They hugged and held the girls.

"And not to be left out are two young lads who should be the inspiration for every adult in this room. They believed they could do something adults could not do, and they convinced their father and grandpa that they would be alright in the process. As you know already, they found the girls, splinted Elizabeth's legs after freeing her from part of a large, downed tree. Then they used survival blankets to keep the soaking wet girls warm throughout the rest of the rainy night."

"And if that wasn't enough, they dove into the strong current of the river, found an unconscious copter crewman, pulled him to the shore and saved his life by doing CPR.

"Wait, I'm not done yet. Captain Ray Hanson rescued the other copter crewman, likewise doing CPR. But the pilot had no heartbeat. The boys then swam back to the copter, found an AED, brought it back to shore and, as you all know, it saved the pilot's life. Ladies and gentlemen, two young men who deservedly are among those who truly would be called heroes tonight, Nathan and Patrick McPherson."

The place went wild. Tears of joy were on the faces of many. For the third time, another standing ovation, with loud cheering. The boys didn't know what to do. They were blushing and felt overwhelmed with all the attention. Ranger Hugh motioned them to stand. They did so, and the clapping became even louder. They quickly sat down and finally everyone became quiet again. No one in that lodge would ever forget the past twenty-six hours and the heroism it revealed.

Ranger Hugh told the gathered campers, rangers, and other park staff that had been off duty and had returned that the St. Croix State Park was officially closed to the public until further notice. He told the group that there would be heavy equipment, loggers with chain saws, carpenters, and laborers to rebuild the buildings. More generators would be brought in to provide power to get more things operational. The ranger told the group he didn't know when electricity would be available again.

"Now, let me say this," continued Hugh, "I've been overwhelmed and touched deeply by how you as campers pitched in to help and care for each other overnight. Many of you spent the night, all night, searching and helping others. Normally, you would be told by the authorities that the park was closed, and you have to leave immediately. However, you obviously are very special people. If you would like to remain to help clean up around here, you are welcome to stay for as long as you would like.

"Talk it over with your loved ones. I have a sign-up sheet here with me for all who would like to stay. It will provide us with your names, campsite location and how long you plan to be here. Every day, there will be a list of projects that you can volunteer for. And yes, you're welcome to relax, fish, swim, and hike."

He then dismissed the campers. The place was buzzing with families talking about what their plans should be, whether to leave or stay and help. It only took the Edwards and Elizabeth seconds to indicate they were going to be on the list to stay and help. The McPhersons didn't have to even discuss it. They sensed it was the right thing to do and joined the Edwards in line to sign Ranger Hugh's sheet.

Twenty-two

The ensuing days after the meeting were spent primarily cleaning up debris. The schedule was rather loosely applied, but generally the rangers wanted the volunteers to help from 9 am to about 3 pm each day. Elizabeth was given use of an older 4-wheeler that one of the maintenance men fixed up for her. She rode around the campground, bringing supplies to the workers and volunteers. Meanwhile, Katrina and the boys teamed up together to work with the loggers in clearing and cleaning up the downed trees. The hardware store in Pine City delivered dozens of pairs of work gloves to the campground.

After their shift was over, the four teens would explore the state park in Elizabeth's 4-wheeler. They would often talk about that night on the steep riverbank and the helicopter crash. Each shared what they remembered and saw as the bird spun erratically and out of control into the river. Patrick remembered what sounded like a gunshot and the panic as they realized the copter might crash down upon them on the steep slope of the bank.

"Hey," said Nate, "I forgot to tell you, I'm a buck richer because of sleeping on the riverbank under the mylar tarp. Something was poking me in the shoulder. I thought it was a rock, but it turned out to be an old silver dollar."

"What? Let's see it," said Elizabeth. As Nate handed her the coin, she gasped. "Nate McPherson, this isn't just any silver dollar. Did you even look at it? Look at the date, 1895. I'll bet this is part of that stolen coin collection. The ranger said the bag had old Morgan Silver Dollars in it and each coin was worth, like, maybe, several hundred thousand. You could be rich."

Elizabeth's declaration prompted the four to conspire secretly to return to the place the helicopter rescued them from. However, the work schedule minimized the times they could go exploring. It was still basically an inaccessible area with all the downed trees across the trails. It was going to take at least a full day to get to the site, excavate, look around, and return before dark. They figured the only possibility for hunting for treasure was going to be during the upcoming weekend. They promised each other they would say nothing about the coin to anyone. It would be their own secret.

Meanwhile, the two families switched off having supper one night at the McPherson campsite and the next at the Edwards. The evenings always ended the same, sitting around a campfire with s'mores.

A friendship was obviously developing between the adults and the teens. Elizabeth was becoming less and less dependent upon her crutches. She told the families gathered around the campfire at the end of their third night that she had a surprise for them. She got up out of her chair and, without using the crutches, walked around the campsite, showing off her new freedom. The two families clapped in celebration.

Twenty-three

Elizabeth was concerned with her newfound ability to walk without crutches that the rangers would take away her favorite 4-wheeler that she had started to think of as her own. But that was not to be the case. Ranger Hugh told her she could use the vehicle while she was at the campground. As a result, it continued to provide transportation for Katrina and the two boys to explore the further reaches of the park.

The weekend finally arrived. The four teens held a pow-wow and decided they would spend Saturday morning with family and then explore during the afternoon on Saturday. Sunday would be spent searching the river rescue spot for the coins.

Elizabeth and Katrina loaded up the 4-wheeler with water and snacks and went across the campground to pick up the boys. They agreed to head toward the group camp, which did not have any campers at the time of the tornado. For that reason, no one really paid much attention to that area of the park. The teens figured they would be the first since the storm to set foot in that area of the park.

They were about a half mile from the main campground when the teens discovered an upside-down canoe. A large, downed pine tree branch held it in place. It had a major dent where the branch was located, and an uncountable number of smaller dents, but otherwise was in usable condition.

"What do you think about trying the canoe out on the river? It might be fun to be on top of the water rather than diving down in it for copter crew rescues," said Patrick. "I think it would hold all four of us. We would only need paddles and life jackets."

"Hey, I saw those things at the camp store when I was bringing mops and buckets to the adults that were cleaning up the mess at the store. I'll bet I could get Ranger Hugh or Ranger Alice to open the building and get us those things," said Elizabeth.

"Hate to be a Debbie-downer here, but anyone think about the fact that we're a long way from both the river and the campground. Don't even think about carrying that thing," said Katrina.

"It's safe to assume," said Patrick, "that the damage when this thing was flying through the air was far more than anything we might do to it by dragging it back to the campground. Besides, the ground is saturated and is really soft. All we have to do is figure out how to tie it up to the 4-wheeler."

"You guys have belts on?" asked Elizabeth. Each did and they put them together to make a strapline from the 4-wheeler to the canoe. It worked perfectly. As they pulled into the campground, canoe in tow, adults seemed to appear from every direction, smiling at the unique sight of a canoe being pulled around by a 4-wheeler. The four dragged their trophy over to the camp store.

One of the campground maintenance men was working on sealing up the damaged roof. A quick request from Elizabeth procured the needed life jackets and paddles. She also garnered a clothesline rope off one of the store shelves again without a problem from the maintenance man. He said he was certain the rangers would see it as a good tradeoff for the teens finding and returning the canoe. The four quickly replaced their belts with the new clothesline rope.

The next half hour was burned up with the four trying to convince their parents that it was okay for the four to go canoeing on the rapidly flowing river. They received approval because there was temporary

cell service and the promise they would meet
Grandpa Al at a designated landing roughly five miles
downstream at 7 pm, well before darkness that
arrived at that time of the year, about 9 pm.

There was one stipulation from Grandpa Al.
He took the boys aside and said only two words, 'be
prepared'. Patrick and Nate instantly knew what he
meant.

Twenty-four

Adults smiled as Elizabeth's 4-wheeler, as it became known around the park, pulled the canoe towards the launch area at the river's edge. Within minutes, the teens had their life jackets on, phones and the familiar backpacks in dry bags, strapped onto the frame of the canoe.

They were off on what they assumed was going to be a quiet ride downriver to the awaiting Grandpa Al.

But it wasn't to be. Within minutes, they spotted pieces of debris from the campground. Camp chairs, picnic tables, and dozens of coolers littered the shallows of the river. Parts of tents, sleeping bags, and clothing were scattered everywhere along the banks.

The beauty of the wilderness looked like a dump instead.

Several miles down the river, Nate said, "Hey, I think this is the area where the copter crashed. Remember that experience? I think Elizabeth described it as the worst date ever. Look, a deer taking a drink at the river's edge."

About the same time, Katrina noticed a bald eagle swooping overhead, ready to do some fishing.

"Now this is more like what I remembered of this place from our trip here last summer," said Nate.

The second he finished his sentence; a gunshot rang out with a splash from the bullet a foot in front of the canoe.

"Pull it over here now or I'll kill you with the next shots," demanded the loud male voice.

Patrick immediately steered the canoe towards the voice on the opposite side of the river from the state park. There wasn't any doubt in his mind that the voice would follow through with his threat, since the shot had been so close to the canoe without hitting it.

As the canoe reached the bank, a large, muscular unshaven man appeared from the dense vegetation. "Get out now!" he demanded. "Lay down face first on the ground and don't move. Well, what do we have here? kiddies out for a ride?"

He monitored the four as he walked over to the canoe and rummaged through dry bags, but was particularly interested in the clothesline that had been used to drag the canoe.

"Perfect." He grabbed the rope and said, "Okay kiddies, it's time for me to enjoy putting an end to your little play date." The guys thought about making a run for it, knowing the man wouldn't be able to catch them both. Yet they worried about what he would do to whomever might not be able to escape his grasp. Patrick decided this was one of those times that Gramps had taught them to be patient and watch for an opportunity. One after another, the man bound the rope around each teen's hands and feet. He pulled the ropes so tight the girls squealed with pain. The guys grunted, not wanting to reveal the hurt nor give the man any more pleasure in subduing his prey.

Once the bindings were complete, the man pushed each of the teens again down on their stomachs again on the wet sand. He put his large boot into the back of Patrick, momentarily knocking the wind out of him. The others could only watch and hope they would not be next to get the boot. The man, now confident he had subdued his captives, returned to the process of looking through the teen's belongings. It only took a second for him to find the phones, which he quickly pitched out into the middle of the river. Communications had now been severed.

While the man was going through the backpacks, Patrick noticed the rifle. It was the same make and model that Gramps had on his farm. He had told them the military and law enforcement were the only people allowed to have the particular firearm. It had metal piercing capability and extreme long-distance accuracy in the hands of a sharpshooter. The light came on in Patrick. Is this what happened to the copter? This guy, the gun, the gunshot, and the crash?

The man dumped the contents of the dry bags on the shore. He grabbed all the energy bars and bottles of water but didn't notice the things Gramps had added to each of the packs as part of Nate and Patrick's preparedness.

"You've done me good, kiddies. We're going to keep each other company until dark and then you and me are going to part ways using your canoe, thank you very much! Kiss your little lives goodbye. You'll be good ole bear food before the night is over and I'll be miles from here and a happy camper." He thought he was making a funny joke using the word camper, but none of the teens gave him the pleasure of even the slightest laugh.

"What do you want with us?" asked Nate, trying to figure out who and why they had been shot at.

"I don't give a hoot about you little pipsqueaks. Just want your transportation. Lost mine days ago and have had to foot it ever since," he replied.

Patrick felt a hint of courage deep within. "Are you the dude that shot down the rescue helicopter?"

"Ya, pretty excellent shot, wasn't it? Suppose you were the kiddies on that slope. Y'all done good saving those copter guys. I was impressed. I didn't really want to kill 'em. Shot 'em down cuz I thought they were looking for me. Didn't even realize they were really after you guys until I watched the rescue of little girlie over there through my scope. When the copter returned, I was sure they were going after me, maybe having seen a reflection or something off my rifle, so I took 'em out."

Surprising everyone, Elizabeth, with attitude, said, "You piece of shit, what you did almost murdered two people who were only responding to do a good thing. What is wrong with you?"

"Well, aren't you a little firecracker? You obviously haven't heard. I guess it's best we keep it that way. Let's just say I'm wanted by the authorities. No one listens to me, though. Been telling the cops I'm innocent ever since I was arrested. But no one listens. I finally had to take matters into my own hands. I'm going to find the actual killer. Enough talk kiddies," as he tore strips from the extra sweatshirt Nate had in his backpack. Then, using the strips, he gagged each of them.

Patrick suddenly felt helpless. He thought about the night on the slope, the helicopter crash, the days he and Nate had with the girls cleaning up the state park, and he wondered if it was all coming to an end. What was this man, who could shoot down a helicopter, going to do to them?

Twenty-five

The man grabbed the ropes on the teen's wrists and pulled them one by one, away from the riverbank up into the dense brush. He didn't worry about them being scraped and scratched by the brush as he yanked on the ropes that bound them. No amount of muffled screaming or crying troubled him.

He made certain there would be no ability for the four to help each other, using the rest of the clothesline to bind each body to a different tree. "Bear food," he laughed and muttered out loud as he finished the confinement of the last of the four. The man knew it was unlikely a bear would even be in the area, especially with all the commotion. He figured he'd use the bear fear to control the teens.

Gagged and tied, the four teens knew there was going to be another all-out search from their parents and probably the rangers as well. But they didn't know if it would be soon enough and if there would still be anyone alive to rescue. The one ace in the hole, the boys thought, was grandpa. He would know there was trouble on the water when they didn't meet per the plan.

Darkness was setting in as Al McPherson used his cell phone to call his son back at the campground. The kids were currently more than an hour late to the landing, the pickup location. They hadn't bypassed the spot by mistake, because Al had gone to the landing an hour earlier than planned, just to make certain he would be visible to the kids.

Jay told his father that he had overheard the rangers having a serious pow wow about a prison break. They told of a convict that had escaped from the prison in the town of Stillwater, a couple of hours south of the state park. He had commandeered a vehicle from an unsuspecting motorist by showing the driver his rifle. "He escaped the morning of the tornado. Looks like he headed north to disappear into the forests. The vehicle was found on the Wisconsin side of the river a few miles south of the state park. A local came upon the car and called the sheriff. The authorities figured he's on foot hiding out in the woods."

"That's not good. Since we don't have canoes, you're going to have to walk the river from the campground. I'll start walking the riverbank from the landing towards you. Get help from the rangers and tell Ranger Hugh he should carry. He'll understand," said Grandpa Al.

Once he had secured the teens, the man walked back to the river and quietly lifted the canoe into the water. He gave it a big push, sending it out into the current. Despite what he had told the teens, there was no way he was going to put himself on display to the authorities in a canoe. Then he walked back into the woods to a large tamarack tree about a stone's throw from his hostages. He sat down and leaned his back up against the tree and peeled open the wrappers on several of the teen's energy bars. The energy bars were gone in a few bites, reminding him of the Hostess Donettes he had lifted from the convenience store on the day of his escape. They were good for a while, but now he was more than starved. Likewise, the energy bars weren't much but were at least something to put into his growling stomach.

He had been on the run from the Stillwater state penitentiary for days and was exhausted. The morning of his escape, he overpowered a guard and, with a solid right forearm to the guard's head, knocked him unconscious. He quickly switched clothes with the guard, picked up his rifle, and used the guard's keys to slip out of the prison. The rifle and the police-looking uniform had helped him commandeer a car to head north. To throw off the authorities, he crossed over into Wisconsin and used county roads to drive to Grantsburg. There he turned on to County Road F towards the St. Croix River

Fearing the possibility of being spotted by the cops, he drove the vehicle into the woods using a small gravel pathway which once served as a logging road. He had heard the tornado warnings on the radio and saw the impending storm brewing. The escapee ditched the vehicle into a deep gully alongside the logging road. It turned out to be the right decision. As the tornado roared through, the force of the wind overturned the car onto its side. The man survived with only bruises.

After the tornado, he left the vehicle on foot and cut through the woods to the river. His original plan was to keep heading north to Duluth, where he thought he could disappear and find the actual killer. But now the kiddies, as he called the four teens, complicated matters. It was time for a new plan.

Katrina was the only one who had any ability to see the man as he ate the energy bars. She wasn't close enough to see the man's eyes, but watched the man's head occasionally bob up and down and then stay down. She guessed he was asleep. As the darkness encompassed the captives. Katrina rubbed her face against the coarse bark of the tree for what seemed like forever before eventually freeing herself from the gag in her mouth. However, freedom came at a cost. The bark drew blood from across her cheeks.

She mouthed to the others, "All ok? I've almost got my wrists free too." Ninety seconds later, she dropped the bindings and slowly moved from body to body, freeing the others. Silently, Nate and Patrick grabbed their empty packs and motioned the girls to hurry away from the man. He did not stir. Patrick led the three straight east, away from the river and into the forest. He thought it was their best chance to evade the man in the darkness. They hiked in what they hoped was the same direction for 20 minutes, stopping only momentarily to listen for footsteps behind them. Patrick figured they were roughly three quarters mile from the man if he was still sleeping. It was a big 'if'.

Not taking any chances, he whispered, "If we head north and then circle back to the river, do you think you could swim across to the other side? I don't think the man would think we'd dare do it in the dark or with the strong current."

Each gave the affirmative. Patrick turned to the left and guided the group in what he assumed was a big circle towards the river. He was hoping they would end up at least a half mile or more north of where the man had tied them to the trees. But they had no way of being certain. Their compasses were back on the riverbank where the man had dumped the contents of their backpacks. They knew they had burned up a lot of energy and another 45 minutes in the darkness.

When they reached the rapidly flowing river, Patrick said, "We must swim quietly, and we must stay together. If you get in any trouble, do not scream out... whisper. Sounds travel long distances at night. Katrina, Elizabeth, do you think you can do this?"

"I'm worried about my legs. They aren't strong, and I've been hurting as we've been going through the woods. But let's go," said Elizabeth.

The girls wondered why Nate and Patrick were wearing their empty backpacks, but didn't ask. Instead, they followed the two into the river. They quietly waded into the cold, rapidly flowing current of the river until the water level reached their necks. The inability to see where they were going, and the muddy feel beneath their feet felt unforgiving. The quickly increasing water depth forced them to swim the rest of the way. It happened as they reached the half-way point across the wide river. Elizabeth, in a muted voice, said, "I can't go any further. My legs won't work anymore."

"Elizabeth, listen to me," said Nate quietly. "You can do this! Float on your back and use your arms to keep yourself moving. I'll be right by your side. Patrick and Katrina keep going.".

The four kept swimming, but Elizabeth was seriously struggling. They were about three quarters of the way across when Elizabeth said, "Help!" and not so quietly. It scared everyone, fearing the man too, heard her plea.

Nate grabbed the arm of the struggling, sinking girl. He got her to float on her back and started to tow her. She could hear him gasping for air as he struggled to swim in the fast-moving current. Gradually they made progress towards the illusive shore. "Help me," he told Elizabeth, "Use your one arm to help."

Patrick and Katrina both heard the commotion and swam back to the struggle and joined in the task of getting Elizabeth to shore. Some minutes later, the exhausted teens reached the steep riverbank. They knew it was probable, in fact likely, that Elizabeth's call for help gave away their location.

Unfortunately, their fear was not unfounded. The loud call had awakened the sleeping escapee a half mile south of the swimmers. He immediately realized he no longer had captives. He stood still, listening, wondering where the sound had come from. Then he turned and moved down into the open along the bank of the river.

"Come on guys," said Nate, whispering, "we've got to hide and get away from the river." Nate helped Elizabeth, while Patrick pulled Katrina up the slope. They found a huge, downed cottonwood tree not unlike what had been torturing Elizabeth's legs earlier in the week.

"We have to hide quickly. I think he might have heard Elizabeth when we were swimming. Get under the branches of that downed tree. We must get completely camouflaged from the man's rifle scope. And we'll need to huddle together to keep warm as well as to minimize the chance the man will see us. If we don't see the man in the daylight, we'll climb the bank and start heading towards the campground," said the eldest.

The guys removed their backpacks and unzipped a compartment and squeezed something that had been sewn into the fabric of the pocket.

"Okay guys, what's the deal with the empty backpacks that you both reached into?" whispered Katrina.

"I think it happened after our last overnight adventure with you two. Remember the one that Elizabeth described as the worst date night ever? Well, Gramps sewed locators into our backpacks. They're like Apple Tags, only much smaller and more sophisticated. By pressing the buttons on the units in our backpacks simultaneously, we alerted Gramps we were ok. It was our way of sending a code and our location without having our phones. It will come up as an alert on his phone and will pinpoint to him our exact location. I think gramps was making sure he could find us without it taking all night to do it."

It didn't go unnoticed by the girls that it was grandpa who had placed the sophisticated locators in the backpacks. It would be a topic to be discussed with the guys at another time.

"Speaking of phones, I'm pissed that mine is now at the bottom of the St. Croix. All my pictures of this very boring camping trip to Minnesota are now only available to the bass and trout in the river," said Katrina, trying to be funny.

"We'll that's not exactly the case," said Nate. "There are a few turtles that might be interested as well. By the way, your pix are safe. They're stored on the cloud, and you can download them when you get a new phone."

"Sorry, I'm still mad. What am I going to do without it for the rest of the trip?" It was a question on each of their minds. Nate and Patrick realized they were going to have to do without until they could earn enough money by working on Gramp's farm to purchase new ones. He had been gracious enough to pay them for working around the farm. Dad and Mom were always keen on the boys earning their own way to buy the stuff many other parents simply gave to their kids. Most of the time, the guys understood and went along with the practice, but being without a phone was going to be hard also on them.

The more Katrina thought about the pictures on her phone, the more upset she became. She realized a fair number of her recent favorites were of the guys, particularly Patrick. She wouldn't admit it to anyone, but she was coming to really like him. He was cute, authentic, and so different from her guy friends back at school. Without the pictures, how would she remember him when she was back in Malibu? Without phones, she wouldn't even be able to talk with him. Now, with all huddled so close, she wanted in the worst way to reach over to grab hold of his hand. But she didn't dare for fear that Patrick didn't share her same feelings.

Twenty-six

At the landing, Grandpa Al opened the truck door and reached into the hidden glove box, using his fingerprint to open the concealed compartment. He retrieved his Glock and his NOGs, his night optical goggles. Though retired, Gramps was still licensed to carry. He doused himself with mosquito repellant and began as silently as possible to walk north on the riverbank. Meanwhile, Jay, Bob Edwards, and the rangers were heading downriver from the campground.

An hour passed as the group of searchers from the campground headed south along the riverbank. It was more than slow going, with the bank being littered with downed trees. In places, the submerged shoreline forced the searchers to wade into the river. Meanwhile, Grandpa Al headed north on the same side of the river from the landing where he was to meet the teens. Theoretically, he or the campground search group should find the teens.

Al was the first to make a discovery. The NOGs helped him to spot the empty canoe floating down the river. He tore off the goggles, stripped out of his boots, and dropped his gun onto the dry bank. He dove into the river and swam out to the canoe. Moments later, with one hand on the canoe and using the other to pull himself through the water, he towed it back to shore.

Back on the riverbank, not wanting to illuminate his location, he covered his phone as he dialed his son and the other searchers. "I have their canoe. It's empty. None of their possessions are in the boat. I'm continuing to move upriver."

He thought of all the reasons the canoe was floating empty. It was dry inside, so it was unlikely that the teens had overturned. Obviously, the teens had beached it somewhere and were on land. Evidently, they had taken their belongings with them. But why was the canoe floating free? There had to be something more to their disappearance. But what?

Unfortunately, the news did nothing to help the spirits of the other searchers coming from the campground. The four teens hiding in the downed tree shivered. The wet clothes and the cool night air took their toll. Patrick broke off leafy branches and laid them over the group as a makeshift blanket. It helped a little, a very little.

Elizabeth whispered, "I hope you guys won't be offended, but I think this night has now taken over as my worst date ever. We might have to re-think the idea of going hunting for the coins. I think this has become enough excitement for one weekend." The other three groaned.

Katrina perked up and said, "At least you won't forget this one."

Grandpa Al continued to move upriver slowly. Less than twenty minutes after his last call to his son, he saw with his NOGs motion on the opposite side of the river. It was a man moving in and out of the woods, almost like he was looking for something. One minute, he was holding the rifle. The next, he was stumbling around without it. It would not take a rocket scientist to deduce the man was the escapee. But where were the kids and did the rifle guy have anything to do with their disappearance?

He stood silently watching the man through his NOGs and followed his motion from across the river. The man was obviously distressed. Suddenly, the man bent over and yelled, "Shit, shit, shit!" His voice carried easily across the river in the darkness. It was a good sign, thought the retired agent.

A second later, his phone beeped twice. The locators. Grandpa Al smiled. The kids were less than a half mile north of his position and across the river from the escapee.

The man now knew his wonderful plan had a flaw. He had heard Elizabeth's cry for help while she was in the river. But he couldn't determine where the cry had originated. He thought the four teens were now somewhere along the river or hiding in the forest that he was to use for his escape. He tried to think like a teen. What would I do if I were in their shoes? He thought they would go upriver towards the campground, via the easiest route, along the shoreline of the river. He stood still on the river's edge to listen for voices or noise from the four. Surely, they would make some kind of commotion hurrying up the shoreline. He would follow and they would not escape a second time.

A shot rang out, then a second. The smile disappeared from his face. The bullets had hit their mark. He moved quickly northward. He was no longer in stealth mode.

Katrina gasped upon hearing the shots. Patrick grabbed her hand and whispered, "Don't move, no noise. Be absolutely still until we figure out what just happened. I don't think he was shooting at us."

Nate was the first to hear the crunch of branches. Someone was coming up the shoreline on their side of the river. The four froze, hoping against hope that it wasn't the man coming after them. Only a moment or two passed before the footsteps were clearly audible. They heard the person's breathing and clothing rubbing against his body. Then he stopped, as if listening for something. A soft voice broke the silence. "Patrick, Nate, Katrina, Elizabeth, it's Gramps!"

The reunion was heartfelt as the retired agent crawled under the branches and hugged each, joining the four in their hiding place. Gramps covered the screen of his phone as he pushed the button to talk to his son. He said quietly, "Jay, I have the kids. I'll bring them back to the campground. Proceed back to the park carefully." The four noted Gramps' low, soft voice, and that he covered the screen with his hand. Despite those actions, the four relaxed. Gramps didn't seem to share that same sense of security.

The retired agent put his NOGs back on and carefully peered out of the branches, looking up and down the river for any movement. He wished he had infrared capability to look for any heat sources. Somewhere out there was a man with a rifle. Gramps laid out the plan. They would sit still for a half hour while he watched through his NOGs and all listened for any sign of the man.

As if on cue, just as gramps was going to give the 'all-clear' sign, he spotted the man across the river walking along the shoreline. The man was obviously on a mission, stopping every minute to listen. Gramps didn't move a muscle. The others immediately realized they needed to do the same, even though they could not see the man in the darkness.

The group remained motionless, with breathing as the only sound and movement. Gramps, with almost imperceptible turns of his head, followed the movement of the man up the shoreline. When he could no longer see the escapee, he whispered it was time to leave their hideout.

Gramps went first out from the cover of the tree, climbing slowly and as quietly as possible up the steep slope. He constantly monitored the opposite riverbank for any movement. Three quarters of the way to the top, he stopped and found cover from a downed tree and again looked through his NOGs. Per plan he gave let out a muted, rodent-like squeak. It was the signal for the first of the teens to leave the nest and climb the slope.

Katrina was the first to pass by Gramps and get to the top of the ridge. She quickly and quietly moved inland and away from the possibility of being seen by the man. The identical process was repeated three more times, each prefaced with the rodent-like squeak.

After sitting still for two minutes after the last of the teens had passed by him, Gramps used the

NOGs to confirm he could join the teens at the top of the embankment. Once they were together again, Gramps led them towards the road and his pickup. It would be a long walk, but no one seemed to care. The teens felt the joy of freedom once again as they followed the footsteps of Grandpa Al.

Epilogue

As the first hints of daylight appeared, the Grandpa Al's pickup entered the campground and parked outside the ranger station. As they entered the office, a gathering of parents and rangers quickly surrounded and hugged the teens. It was a celebration reminiscent of the girls being found alive after the tornado.

The teens gave a synopsis of their canoe trip. It was déjà vu. The teens were again safe after another terrifying experience. The Edwards held Katrina and Elizabeth in their arms. It looked as though they would never let go. Jay and Grandpa Al hugged Patrick and Nate. Elizabeth told the adults how Patrick had led them through the woods and how

Nate had helped her get across the river. The Edwards hugged the guys and once again thanked them profusely.

The adults in the room at that moment sensed they were in the presence of special and courageous teenagers.

Patrick, enjoying the moment, tried to add a note of humor, suggesting it was time for everyone to catch 40 winks before sunrise. It was all that was needed to get everyone to head out of the ranger's office with a smile on their faces. The teens knew their camping adventure was not over. The coins were yet to be found. But they were certain after tonight's episode, they were going to have to do some sweet talking if they were to get out of their parent's sight ever again. However, at that very moment, everything seemed right with the world and that was all that mattered.

Gramps, however, was not under the impression that everything was peaches and cream at that instant and didn't exit the office with the rest of the group. He held back and caught the eye of Ranger Hugh, motioning him to stay. When they were face to face, the senior McPherson said only four words to the ranger. "We have a problem."

The End

The shots found their mark. But what or who was the target and why? Who was the shooter? Does the escaped convict reappear? Whatever happened to the coins? Together Patrick, Katrina, Nate, and Elizabeth continue their adventure in book two of the series at your favorite bookseller soon.

About the Author

Miller, as a lifelong camper, has pitched his tent in a multitude of states and types of topography. Through years of directing canoe and camping trips, he has had the privilege of introducing many students to secluded forests and crystal-clear lakes. His camp journals and photos continue to fuel his imagination for his writings.